ALL THE COMFORTS OF HOME...

Jessie went into the hotel and climbed the stairs to her room on the second floor. While she and Ki had been out, the chambermaids had been busy. Her bed had been remade, her toilet articles rearranged neatly on the chiffonier.

As she glanced around the room, she saw only one thing that was at odds with its neatness. At the broad double window, one of the curtains was wrinkled and awry. Jessie stepped to the window and lifted the curtain—and froze.

Four sticks of dynamite had been hidden by the heavy drapery.

2.00

WESLEY ELLIS

LONE STAR

AND THE
SHADOW CATCHER

JOVE BOOKS, NEW YORK

LONE STAR AND THE SHADOW CATCHER

A Jove Book / published by arrangement with
the author

PRINTING HISTORY
Jove edition / December 1989

ISBN: 0-515-10194-X

PRINTED IN THE UNITED STATES OF AMERICA

10 9 8 7 6 5 4 3 2 1

Chapter 1

"If I remember what Ed Wright said yesterday, there's just a little holding herd in that pasture we're coming to, Ki," Jessica Starbuck called over her shoulder.

"That's right," Ki replied. "Eight or ten steers is what he said, not more than that."

Jessie had reined Sun to a walk, waiting for Ki to catch up with her. Now she lowered her voice as he reached her side.

"Sun hasn't had enough galloping to work off his restlessness," she went on. "If you'll push ahead of me and open the fence, I'll give him a good run the rest of the way to the gate and all the way across the next pasture to the line fence. You can either catch up with me or wait until I turn back."

Ki acknowledged Jessie's request with a wave. He dug the heels of his sandals into the flank of the big bay he was riding. The horse responded at once by spurting past Jessie and Sun, heading for the make-do gate that broke the strands of barbed wire.

It was the kind of simple temporary gate used on most Texas ranches, one that a cowhand could fabricate on the spot and that could be made quickly and

1

handled easily by one man. Three ten-foot strands of barbed wire had been looped at equal spaces around two slim posts and twisted firmly in place to form the gate. It was held in place by doubled loops of wire bent around the permanent fence posts at their tops and bottoms.

Ki had only to slip the top loop off the nearest end post and lift the bottom end free. Then he dragged the gate aside, and Jessie toed Sun through the gap. She let the reins go slack and dug her heels into Sun's flanks. The palomino responded with a burst of speed, its hooves digging into the short grass as it moved forward with a sudden thrust of its muscular hind-quarters.

Jessie threw her head back and let her wide-brimmed hat drop until it was caught on her back by its long loose chin strap. Bending forward, she tattooed gently with her heels on Sun's barrel. The big palomino seemed to have been waiting for her signal. The tempo of its hooves on the short-grassed soil became a steady drumbeat as Sun responded to Jessie's silent urging with a burst of speed before settling down to a leg-stretching gallop that took them in a straight line toward the little ridge that topped the rise.

Halfway up the rise the breeze that had not reached the bottom of the hollow lifted Jessie's golden hair and it rippled in a sunkissed glow behind her in the light breeze that brushed her face as Sun carried her up to the crest. On the grassed level ground beyond the ridge a small bunch of cattle grazed.

Jessie lifted her hand to tighten the reins and head Sun away from the grazing steers, but in the close ties that bound them together the palomino had already anticipated her intention. It angled away from the

2

steers long before there was any danger that a collision with one of the animals could cause it to break its stride.

Turning her eyes away from the level grassed downslope, Jessie glanced at the steers. The little bunch had stopped its leisurely grazing when Jessie and Sun broke over the crest of the ridge, but now the steers were beginning to scatter out again. Jessie counted nine of them before turning her head back to look more closely at one steer which had not moved with its fellows. The animal had not changed its stance since Jessie first noticed it. The steer stood with its legs apart, its head down and swaying gently.

Jessie frowned, but did not tighten the reins because Sun was now careening along at full tilt on the downslope beyond the crest. In the distance she could see the Circle Star's line fence, perhaps two miles ahead. Though it was a bit farther than she'd thought, she decided to give Sun his head all the way to the fence. Settling firmly into her saddle, Jessie bent forward, enjoying the gallop as much as did the palomino.

Once again the big black stallion dropped out of its gallop without waiting for Jessie to rein it in as the shining strands of barbed wire rose ahead. A few moments later it reached the fence and stopped. Jessie took the slack out of the reins and sat for a moment, enjoying the memory of the gallop. She looked back along the rise and saw that Ki had reined in just below the crest and was dismounting.

Recalling her fleeting glimpse of the sick steer as Sun had carried her past the place where Ki had now stopped, Jessie toed the palomino around and set it moving at a walking gait toward the spot where she now saw Ki.

He'd dismounted and left his horse a dozen yards or so away while he walked up to the steer to inspect it. He was still looking at the swaying animal when Jessie got within speaking distance, but when he heard the thudding of Sun's hooves he turned and gestured toward the steer. As far as Jessie could tell at a cursory look, it had not moved since she'd raced past it on Sun.

"I noticed there was something wrong with that steer when I rode by it," she said when she reined in. "But Sun was moving a bit fast right then, so I didn't stop. Have you had time to give it a close look?"

"Enough of a look to worry me just a bit," Ki nodded. "See if you agree with me."

Jessie was dismounting while Ki spoke. She stepped up to the steer. It was still standing in the position it had been holding when she rode by it. One look at its drooping head, its dangling tongue and glazed eyes, its widespread legs and the slight swaying of its body told her all that she needed to know.

"If you're thinking locoweed, I'd say you're right," she told Ki as she started toward him.

"It's showing all the symptoms," he agreed.

"I thought the hands had cleared every bit of that miserable marijuana out of all the Circle Star range last year," Jessie said, frowning. "But it looks as though they missed a patch somewhere close around here."

"That's the same idea I had," Ki replied. "But if I've ever seen a marijuana-locoed steer, it's this one we're looking at right now."

Their attention had been drawn from the steer while Jessie and Ki talked. Neither of them had noticed that the animal's look of glaze-eyed helplessness had van-

4

ished or that it had raised its head and was swinging its widespread horns. Jessie's eyes glimpsed the steer's motion first, and when she saw the beast it was raising its head, its glazed eyes glistening redly, its tail switching.

Before she could call a warning, the steer dropped its head again, snorting loudly, and lunged with amazing swiftness, heading for Ki. As it bolted full-speed, it began swinging its wide, threatening horns, their needle-sharp tips glistening in the sunshine. Ki had been standing only an arm's length from the locoed steer. He saw his danger in time to leap back, but the distance was too small and the steer's forward lunge too fast and too totally unexpected.

Reaching Ki, the big animal set its hooves in a sliding stop and swung its drooping head. The speed with which it moved had been very deceptive. When it brought its head sweeping around, the wickedly pointed tip of crazed steer's horn did not stab into Ki's flesh when the steer set its hooves in a sliding stop and swung its drooping head; the needle-sharp tip of one horn slid like a swordsman's blade through the rippling folds in the fabric of Ki's jacket. The tip pierced the closely-woven cloth as easily as the needle point it resembled would have gone through a sheet of taut tissue paper.

So sudden and deceptive were the steer's moves that for the fraction of a second Ki did not even realize his jacket had been caught on the horn. Then the animal suddenly raised its swinging head and began to turn. The few inches of play between the steer's massive head and the curve of its horn closed. The cloth of Ki's jacket twisted like the loop of a lasso, pulling his arms to his ribs and holding them there like a giant

5

grasping fist. The steer raised its once-drooping head and Ki suddenly found himself being lifted off his feet.

As the steer's head went up in a half-turn and reached the end of the arc in which it was moving, Ki was dragged along the short span until he was sprawling with his head down on the animal's broad muzzle. He kicked out strongly, trying to break free, but with every kick his head jarred the steer's muzzle and its tender sensitive nose. When it collided with Ki's dangling head, the steer swung its own head more wildly. Its movement pulled Ki closer and bound the jacket's stout fabric as tightly as though it was a straitjacket being strapped closed, to hold him more firmly in place.

Ki twisted as best he could, and kicked hard with his sandaled feet at the bump made by the steer's shoulders, but he might as well have been pounding on hard earth. Balanced and held as he was, both arms useless in the constriction of the jacket's thick closely woven fabric, his feet unable to hold any position on the animal's back, Ki found himself held helpless in a posture which at the moment made his skill at the Oriental martial arts useless.

Though Jessie had drawn her Colt when the steer first moved, she could find no target. Ki's imprisoned shoulders covered the top of the steer's head, ruling out a quick-killing shot into the animal's brain. Jessie knew that by dropping to her knees, she would be in position for a clean shot into the steer's heart, but she also knew that the animal would not die instantly.

Even in the few seconds that would pass after the bullet tore through its heart, the unpredictable moves of the steer's dying throes might hurt Ki badly, might crush his ribs or crack his spine. She stood poised to move in any direction offering a chance to make the shot she needed at an angle that would send a bullet into the soft folds of thin flesh behind the steer's jaws and bring instant death to the crazed animal.

Until the opportunity for such a shot was offered, she could only stand looking at Ki in his helpless position, holding her Colt ready as she racked her brain for another quick solution to her dilemma and found none while precious seconds ticked away.

Jessie knew the habits of steers. She'd learned them of necessity, by the years of experience gained after she'd been forced by her father's murder to take hold of the Circle Star and run it. Among the many things she'd learned was that the actions of a normal animal and one gripped by the effects of locoweed were not the same. What a locoed steer might do was totally unpredictable.

Jessie reached a solution to her problem only a few seconds after she realized that Ki was unable to help himself. The tightened fabric of his jacket immobilized him almost completely. Only his legs were free, and they were kicking in midair as he tried to break free from what had become a binding prison.

Dropping flat on the sloping ground, Jessie fixed her eyes on the steer as it swung its head from side to side, the mighty muscles of its neck and shoulders holding Ki in place. Blinded in one eye by Ki's chest, the steer began to shift position, swinging its head from side to side as it stomped wildly with its forefeet.

Holding her Colt ready, Jessie ticked off the seconds without realizing that she was doing so, waiting for the instant that would give her the necessary angle. Though the time seemed to pass with the slowness of cold molasses being poured from a jug's narrow neck, only a few moments flashed by before the steer began swinging its head from side to side, half-blinded.

At last it shifted its hooves and took a step forward. Jessie waited for its second wary step. It came just as the animal brought up its head again, trying desperately to rid itself of Ki's blinding unwieldy form. In the fraction of a second that passed before it began working its neck and shoulders into a reverse turn that would expose the full stretch of its head and neck, Jessie saw her chance.

For an instant the steer's head was angled away from her, and Jessie triggered a shot from her Colt. The revolver's heavy slug plowed into the steer's neck just behind its curved jaw and followed the exact angle needed to pass on into the animal's brain. For an instant or two the steer swayed. Then its forelegs crumpled and it pitched forward as it fell to the ground.

Even in the quick broken glimpses he'd caught of her, Ki had understood what Jessie was planning when she dropped prone. He was ready as the steer began its slow crumpling fall, and bent his head as far forward as possible. His arched shoulders took the brunt of the impact when the steer's big head dropped to the hard soil, but his arms and torso were still immobilized by the tightly wound blouse. It wrapped him like a straitjacket, holding his upper body trapped and motionless.

"I'm afraid I'm going to need a hand to get out of this trap I'm in," he told Jessie. His voice was as casual as if he were asking her to pass the biscuits at breakfast.

Jessie was already on her feet; she'd started to stand up the moment she saw that her shot had been effective. She stepped up to the dead steer's horns, and by exerting all of her considerable strength managed to lever its unwieldy head around until Ki could roll along the horn that was trapping him and free his jacket from it.

Ki straightened up, stretching his cramped arms in *Sanchin-tachi* moves and bending his legs in the *heiko-tachi* exercises which are used by martial arts experts to relax their limbs and keep their muscles supple and responsive. He ran through the entire roster of the exercises until ending them with the *kake-ashi-tachi* stance and recovery before he stepped up to Jessie.

"That was a very brave shot you took," he told her.

"No." Jessie shook her head. "It wasn't bravery, Ki. It was just the only chance I had to kill that locoed steer without hurting you. I knew the steer's skull would deflect my bullet so that it wouldn't reach you. But that's finished, except for sending a couple of the men up here to drag the carcass off."

"And we'll have to look around and find where that marijuana it grazed on is growing," Ki added. "The men who come to pick up the carcass can clean up the patch while they're here."

"There'll be plenty of time to take care of that," Jessie said. "I can't think of anything that's going to take us away from the Circle Star in the immediate future."

"Things do seem to be running smoothly," he nodded. "We really don't have much to worry about except the roundup, and that's quite a while ahead."

"I'll be glad to—" Jessie began, then stopped as a shout from the distance reached them.

"Hey-oo, Miss Starbuck! If you and Ki don't mind waiting up a minute or so, I'll ride back with you to the main house!" a man's voice called.

"Why, that's Ed," Jessie said as she and Ki turned to look in the direction from which the shout had come.

Ki nodded. "We'll wait for him to catch up. It'll save him and the men time if Ed knows exactly where to find the steer carcass."

"I'd forgotten that this is his day to go to the siding for the mail," Jessie went on. "And that means it's my day to spend going through it."

Mail for the Circle Star was allowed to accumulate at the Southern Pacific's railroad siding for a day or more before someone from the ranch rode in to pick it up. In the early days of the Circle Star, when Alex Starbuck was putting the vast spread together by purchasing a half-dozen smaller ranches, he'd established the informal routine of picking up the mail. It had now come to be a ranch custom.

Though the railroad had offered to build a spur to the Circle Star's main house, Alex had refused. He had no intention of letting a railroad intrude on the privacy that he'd sought by placing his home at the heart of the ranch. The Circle Star had been intended by Jessie's father to be a refuge from the business affairs which absorbed his attention every moment he spent in his San Francisco headquarters.

Alex Starbuck's huge and far-reaching industrial and financial empire had been created in the city of the Golden Gate. After the death of his beloved wife in childbirth, Alex had entrusted Jessie's care to an old retired geisha whom he'd known during his early business career as an importer of Far Eastern goods. Even before Jessie's birth, he'd seen the need for such a place. He'd envisioned owning a haven where he could escape the constant frenzied activity required by his widely scattered business interests.

On a trip to Texas he'd discovered the vast reaches of its rolling hills and broad expanses of prairie. Later, after a great deal of searching other parts of the United States, he'd settled on the open spaces of Southwest Texas as the place where he could find the privacy he needed. He'd begun buying land there, and had devoted much time to creating the immense ranch.

Alex Starbuck's business career had begun in a tiny shop selling Oriental import goods on the San Francisco waterfront. Audacious by nature, Alex had built the little bayside store into an empire. His holdings had grown to include banking, stockbrokerage, financing and mining, manufacturing, shipping and ship-building, lumbering in several huge areas of virgin forests, vast acres of farmland which he leased to individual farmers, and business buildings in the West Coast's larger cities.

When he was in his offices in San Francisco, Alex had enjoyed no rest at all, for during the last years of his busy life he'd devoted much of his time to smashing a vicious cartel. The cartel had its roots in Central Europe, but its branches spread into the Far East as well as Scandinavia. Alex had been invited to become a member of the cartel, but after learning that the sinister group's intention was to gain control of the key businesses of the United States, he became its bitter enemy.

Ki had been Alex's good right arm in the battle against the cartel. Son of a Japanese mother and an American naval officer who'd been one of Alex's life-long friends, Ki had been shut out of the life of his mother's aristocratic family because of his mixed heritage. He'd spent his formative years roaming aimlessly from one of the masters of Oriental martial arts to another.

Alex had discovered the son of his old friends by accident and had offered Ki a home in America. In time Ki had come to be Alex's indispensible helper, and he'd remained with Jessie after her father's untimely death in a hail of bullets from a cartel execution squad.

Although he'd had been away from the ranch when the cartel's killers staged the ambush in which Alex was murdered, Ki stayed with Jessie as her guardian and protector. At the time of her father's death, Jessie had been in her last year at an exclusive New England finishing school for young ladies. She took over Alex's fight against the cartel, and with Ki's constant help the sinister group had been destroyed.

Having grown to young maturity on the Circle Star and later as the mistress and owner of the vast spread, Jessie had worked hard at mastering the skills and acquiring the knowledge needed to run the vast spread. To her as well as to Ki, the sprawling spread would always be home.

Sitting in their saddles beside the dead steer, Jessie and Ki had waited for the Circle Star foreman to reach them. He reined in and looked at the carcass stretched out on the waving prairie grass.

"Looks like it went loco on you," he said, frowning. "But I'd bet just about anything I got that the boys cleared away all of them marijuana weeds."

"They must've missed a few," Jessie replied. "But you can get three or four of them together tomorrow and have them get rid of the carcass and search every inch of this part of the range until they find those marijuana plants and dig them out."

12

"I sure will, Miss Starbuck," Wright said, nodding. He leaned forward and lifted the soft leather mailbag off his saddle horn as he went on: "I'll just hand this over to you now. It's funny, but as many times as I've rode to pick up the mail, it sorta makes me nervous to carry it."

Jessie frowned. "That's odd; you're the foreman, and you sort the mailbag when Ki and I aren't here."

"Foreman or not, I wouldn't presume to go through the mail, Miss Starbuck. Not unless you and Ki was both to be away from the Circle Star. Then's the only time I look at all the letters and pick out what few's addressed to the boys."

"I'll relieve your mind, then," Jessie said, smiling as she took the mail pouch and hung it on her saddle-horn. "Now, suppose we start for the main house. If we don't hurry, we'll be late for supper, and Gimpy will be mad at all three of us."

Chapter 2

"I think we've got some sort of problem developing up in Dakota Territory," Jessie told Ki as she looked up from the letter she'd just finished reading. "Or perhaps it's already developed."

She was sitting at the desk that had once been Alex's, the mailbag open in front of her. She held a thin sheaf of paper in one hand, a single sheet in the other. Ki was in one of the deep leather-upholstered armchairs that stood in front of the now-fireless hearth. He was honing one of his *shuriken* with a small hand whetstone; a stack of the blades that still needed attention were on a table beside him.

He'd looked up from the job he was doing when Jessie spoke. Now he asked, "What sort of problem?"

"I'm not sure, Ki. In fact, I'm not all that sure there is one, because I'm still trying to puzzle out the answer." She held up her hands to show Ki the papers in them, then went on: "You see, one of these letters contradicts the other, and that just doesn't make any sense."

"There are quite a few things about this world that don't make sense to me. What's your puzzle, Jessie?"

"These letters from Bismarck that were in the mailbag that Ed brought today," she replied. "One is from Bob Stevens, the other's from a man named Elzey Pendergast."

Ki frowned. "It's not like Bob to write anything but short and very sensible letters. He's been your supervisor in Dakota Territory for a long time. In fact, he's been up there for so long that I've forgotten when Alex hired him."

"I couldn't tell you that, either, not without going through a lot of old ledgers. But if I'm right, Bob started to work for Alex when the shipyard was first opened. The coal mine and barges came later."

"Which brings us to the second letter," Ki suggested.

Jessie nodded. "I've never heard of this Pendergast, Ki. But his letter's like some that I've gotten from other people. He has some ideas about buying out the properties in Bismarck."

"How does that connect with Bob's letter?"

"It doesn't," Jessie answered. "And Pendergast doesn't say a word about Bob, though I'm sure Bismarck's not so big by now that they wouldn't know each other."

"Then why are you so concerned about them?"

"More confused than concerned," she answered. "One reason is that Bob sent me a preliminary statement of operating figures for the first six months of this year. He's never done that before, and now I'm wondering why he did this time."

Ki said thoughtfully, "There must be some kind of reason, Jessie. Are the figures good or bad?"

"Just about average," Jessie replied. "All three

show a reasonable profit, even though wages have gone up."

"Then I'd say that it's good news overall."

"Yes, of course. The riverboats haven't brought in as much as they used to, but I can understand that. The Northern Pacific's back in full operation after about six years, so the boats have lost some of the loads they carried while the railroad was closed down, or almost closed down."

"But that business will come back if the Northern gets into trouble again," Ki said. "And both of us know that the NP's been having trouble off and on for several years."

"Yes, it's been chancy," Jessie agreed. "It seems to be settling down this time, though."

"Getting back to the letters," Ki went on, "you still haven't said what it is about them that bothers you."

"Aside from wondering why Bob sent these reports, I'm not as puzzled by them as I am by Pendergast's letter. You were in Bismarck with Alex when he was developing those properties. Do you remember having met him?"

Ki shook his head. "As far as I can remember, Alex never had any dealings with anyone by that name. What's his letter about?"

"Well, he starts out by mentioning that some sort of club or workman's guild called the Friends of the Working Man is making trouble at the coal mine and shipyard as well as some of the other businesses in Bismarck."

"What kind of trouble?"

"Reading between the lines of Pendergast's letter, I got the idea that these Friends of the Working Man is a new organization very much like a union, since it's supposed to help workmen get higher wages."

"You shouldn't have any problem with it, then," Ki said. "Alex always paid good wages and you have, too."

"Yes, I know," Jessie agreed. "But that isn't the only thing that bothers me about Pendergast's letter. First he says that besides the other things he's mentioned, barge traffic in the river's been falling off. Then he tells me that he's interested in buying the mine and the barges and the shipyard."

"Somehow that doesn't quite make sense," Ki objected. "Who would want to buy three businesses if they're in trouble?"

Jessie smiled. "Apparently Mr. Pendergast does, or he wouldn't've written me."

"Then whatever decision you make has to be yours."

"What's more to the point is how the figures Bob sent me on the mine's operation can be right if there's all the trouble in Bismarck that this Pendergast mentions in his letter."

"Yes, when you put it that way it doesn't make much sense," Ki said thoughtfully. "Though I know that Alex sometimes bought out businesses that were in bad shape and made them well again."

"I'm not as talented as Alex," Jessie said. "But there's something in this letter from Pendergast that bothers me, even if I can't put my finger on it."

"You get enough strange mail from strange people that you should be able to recognize a fraud when you run into one," Ki suggested.

"Oh, I'm sure this man Pendergast—whoever he may be—isn't a fraud," Jessie said quickly. "But my hunch is that he'd only be interested in buying those

Dakota Territory properties if he could get them at a bargain price."

"Which you don't propose to give him?"

"If the figures Bob Stevens sent me are right, I'd have no reason to sell any of them. You and I both know that Alex never sold a business when it was having problems. He'd cure the problems and then if he wasn't satisfied he'd look for a buyer."

"True," Ki agreed. "So what are you planning to do?"

"I don't like mysteries, Ki," Jessie replied. "And these two letters have mystified me. I think the best thing for us to do is go to Bismarck and find out exactly what's going on."

"It'll be good to get away from smoke and cinders for the rest of our trip," Jessie said.

"And it'll be very enjoyable to have a cabin, even if it's not much bigger than a matchbox," Ki told her. "I'm not very fond of railroad car berths. About all that can be said for them is that they're better than sitting up in a passenger coach all night."

"And a great deal more comfortable than sleeping on a bedroll on the bare ground somewhere," Jessie reminded him.

Jessie and Ki were standing on the narrow walkway that ringed the upper deck of the *Josephine*, watching the last few passengers crossing the gangplank from the levee to the steamboat's lower deck. A handful of people dotted the levee, trying to keep clear of the roustabouts who were wheeling high-stacked dock carts and suitcase-piled dollies up the freight gangplank in a steady stream.

A thin thread of smoke trickled from the sternwheeler's high stacks and trailed back above the block of passenger cabins that filled most of the upper deck behind the narrow slit of the wheelhouse. Everywhere that Jessie looked on the lower deck, neat stacks of cordwood were arranged in head-high piles.

"I'd better go find our cabins," Ki told her. "They said at the office down below that somebody would put our luggage in them, and I'd hate to find that it had been left behind."

"Go ahead," Jessie said. "It's been a long while since I've been on a river steamer, and I'd like to look around a bit."

After Ki had left, Jessie soon grew tired of watching the changing but repetitive activity on the dock. She started toward the vessel's bow and found the narrow passageway between the wheelhouse and passenger cabins. She started through the narrow passageway, heading toward the opposite side of the vessel to look out across the broad expanse of the Missouri River.

Jessie's move took her through the narrow aisle between the block of passenger cabins and the wheelhouse. She glanced into the shallow cramped enclosure that spanned the front of the upper deck just in time to see one of the two men inside it reach for the lanyard that looped from the top of the curved ceiling. He pulled the loop taut and the low-baritone toot of the vessel's whistle filled the air. A second pull, shorter than the first, brought a repetition of the sound.

Shouts sounded from the docks and the *Josephine*'s deck. The bow of the vessel moved slowly ahead. Now the man who'd pulled the lanyard gave all his attention to the head-high wheel that rose between him and the broad expanse of glassed windows. He braced his feet and spread his arms to grasp one of the protruding

19

wheel handles in each hand. Looking beyond him at the river, Jessie saw the *Josephine*'s prow swing slowly toward the middle of the broad placidly flowing river.

After moving on past the wheelhouse, Jessie stood gazing at the busy surface of the Missouri. It was dotted with craft of all shapes and sizes, from low-lying barges piled with bales and boxes to small rowboats that darted in and out between the bigger vessels like oversized water bugs. While Jessie was looking at the unfamiliar vista, Ki came out of the narrow passage between the cabins and the wheelhouse and stopped beside her.

"All our luggage seems to have found its way to our cabins," he said. "So now all that we have to do is relax and rest until we step off the boat at Bismarck."

"I don't know how I'll feel by then," Jessie replied. "But right now, I'm enjoying traveling without the click of rails or the thunking of horses' hooves. Even the splashing of the wheel sounds good; it seems to be part of the river."

"We'll have three days to enjoy it," Ki said. "But if I know you, Jessie, you'll spend a good part of those three days trying to sort out what's behind all the little reasons that got us started to Bismarck."

"I'm past that stage, Ki. I thought about the Bismarck problems a lot on the train to Kansas City, and I don't intend to think of them again until we get off this boat."

Before Ki could answer, a man's voice came from behind them. He said, "Then perhaps you'd be inclined to give a little of your time and attention to me, Jessie."

Jessie and Ki turned at the same time. It was Jessie

who spoke first. "Joe Foreman! Where has the army been hiding you?"

"Oh, in quite a number of places. Unluckily, none of them was as close to the Circle Star as Fort Duncan," the blue-uniformed man who'd come up behind them replied. "And the place that I'm billeted to now is even farther away, so I hope you'll have some time to spare for me on our trip upriver."

"Of course I will!" Jessie assured him.

"I won't hurt your feelings if I take up a lot of Jessie's time, will I, Ki?" Foreman asked, turning to Ki.

"Not at all. While you and Jessie are catching up on old times, I'll be exploring the boat and finding out about this part of the river," Ki replied. "In fact, I think now's a good time to start, while you and Jessie get acquainted again."

As Ki started away, Foreman turned back to Jessie and said, "I didn't want to risk embarrassing you in front of Ki—"

"By kissing me," Jessie broke in. "I wouldn't've been, but that's neither here nor there, now that we have the deck to ourselves."

Foreman did not need a second invitation. He bent forward and sought Jessie's lips. Their kiss of greeting turned into something more as their tongues met and entwined. Foreman's arms were around her now, and they held the kiss until both were breathless. At last their lips parted, and they stood apart, their eyes locked.

Foreman broke the silence that followed their kiss. He said, "You don't know how many times I've thought about you since I was transferred from Fort Duncan, Jessie."

"I'm flattered, Joe," she said, smiling. "But surely

the army's kept you too busy to allow much time for you to think about the past."

"Far from it. I've been stationed at so many isolated outposts that I've had nothing much to think about except the past. I'm not just paying you an empty compliment when I say that the memory of you and those few days we had together when I was stationed in Texas—well, this boat isn't as isolated as that sandy stretch of shore along the Rio Grande, but I can't believe I'm lucky enough to've run into you again."

"My ranch in Texas isn't exactly a busy crossroads," Jessie said with a smile. She'd also been remembering an afternoon beside a river several years ago. "It's isolated, too. But the nice thing about a riverboat is that it has cabins."

"You mean that you'd—"

"Why don't you just come right out and ask me?"

Foreman smiled and clicked his heels together as he drew himself into the position of attention. He said, "Miss Starbuck! Will you do me the honor of paying a visit to my cabin—or yours, if you prefer."

Jessie nodded. "Whichever is the nearest."

"Mine is the one just ahead. I was on my way there when I saw you and Ki standing here."

Jessie tucked her arm into his elbow as she asked, "What are we waiting for, then?"

Two or three steps took them to the cabin. Foreman opened the door and held it for Jessie to enter. With the sun slanting down in the west, the tiny window high in the square cabin's wall brought only a thin trickle of light into the little room. There was barely room for them to stand between the door and the edge of the bunk, which with a small, round cane-bottom chair was all the room contained in the way of furniture.

Jessie turned to face Foreman. As she moved she spread her arms and he stepped up to her, his own arms wide. They clung for a moment in a tight embrace, then Jessie tilted her head back to meet his lips. Their tongues twined in the deep kiss of lovers, and neither of them made any effort to break it until both were breathless.

When their lips parted, Foreman did not release Jessie from his embrace, but Jessie raised her hands to stroke his cheeks and chin with her fingertips. He let his arms slide down her sides and clasped his hands around her rounded buttocks, pulling her to his groin. Despite the barrier of their clothing, Jessie could feel the pressure of his swollen shaft.

"I'm as ready for you as you are for me," she said softly, breaking their kiss and whispering breathlessly into his ear. "But hadn't we better wait until tonight?"

"No," Foreman said firmly. "We'll have tonight, of course, but we've got a chance now, so let's take it."

Jessie did not argue. Her inner turmoil was urging her to grasp the moment. She replied, "All right. Just let go of me long enough for me to get my clothes out of the way."

Reluctantly, Foreman let his arms fall. Jessie lifted the folds of her close-draped traveling skirt and began pulling at the bow-knots that secured the waistband of her pantalets. She glanced at Foreman and saw that he was busy pushing his trousers down his hips. The bulge of his erection formed a promising hump in the veed leg of his thin summer long johns.

ˉ He looked up at her as she turned to stand half-facing him and reached for his swollen crotch. Before

23

Foreman could move, her fingers were on the single button that secured the undergarment and her hands slipped inside the thin fabric to grasp him and free his erection. She stroked its throbbing length for a moment before shifting her feet to turn around in the small span of space between the edge of the bunk and the door.

Jessie lifted her skirt and shift as she turned. She kneeled on the edge of the bunk. Her pantalets were down to her knees now, and she worked them farther down, to the calves of her legs, in order to spread her knees wider.

Foreman stepped up to her while she was bending forward, angling herself on the narrow bunk in order to spread her knees wider apart. Even before she leaned forward to bring her softly rounded buttocks high, Foreman had stepped behind her and was rubbing the warm moist tender nest between her thighs with the throbbing tip of his erection.

Jessie reached back to help him place the head of his shaft and he drove into her. She gasped as she felt him filling her. Twisting her hips for a moment, her sighs became gasps of pleasure as he drove in. She bent farther forward and placed her head on her forearms as her lover began to drive.

"Slower!" she gasped, "I want to feel you in me just as long as you can keep going!"

Foreman did not answer, but he responded to Jessie's breathless request. He'd passed his first frenzy now, and settled down to a steady pace. Jessie was already responding to his long measured lunges as thrust followed lusty thrust.

Small sudden shudders were beginning to ripple through her body, and part of her mind had started urging her to let them carry her with them, but Jessie's experience told her another story. Foreman was beginning to drive faster, and Jessie knew that his body was sending him the same signals that were coming from hers.

Half-turning her head, she said, "Don't hurry, Joe. We don't want this to end too soon."

"I don't want it to end at all," Foreman said. "I'm enjoying it as much as you are."

He slowed the rhythm of his deep penetrations to a more leisurely pace. Instead of lunging, he thrust deliberately. His hands tightened involuntarily on her hips at the end of each long deliberate stroke and he pulled her buttocks to his groin, buried deep within her as he held her firmly against him.

Jessie's urgency ebbed with Foreman's response to her words. The ripples that had been running through her body caught her more often, but the pleasure they brought her did not diminish. She quivered each time he ended a thrust and while her striving for fulfillment had not lessened she still controlled her urgency in spite of the instinctive tensing that involuntarily followed each of her lover's deep slow penetrations.

Time seemed to race and at the same moment to stand still as Foreman maintained the slow steady rhythm he'd fallen into after Jessie's plea. As the minutes ticked away Jessie's urgency grew greater. She realized that her lover was reaching the same point of no return that was sweeping over her with increasing speed.

Jessie broke the silence in the cramped little stateroom with a whisper. She asked, "Are you as ready as I am?"

"Readier, I imagine," Foreman answered. Though

his voice was level, its tone showed his strain.

"Then let's enjoy the ending," Jessie said.

Foreman needed no urging. He speeded up the tempo of his lunges, though their lustiness did not diminish. Jessie was panting now and her body began quivering. She began rotating her hips as best she could in her crouched posture, and now she did not try to suppress the ripples that ran through her body.

Shudder followed shudder, each rippling spasm more violent than the last. Jessie heard Foreman's guttural moan as his strong hands gripped her hips even tighter than before and as he tried to pull her even closer to his groin she could feel his spastic shuddering.

Then Jessie was quivering also in her final exploding frenzy and Foreman's moan died away to a soft sigh while she shuddered and tossed and the muscles that had been so tautly stretched let go and she sagged in Foreman's grasp while he still held her to him until they both grew still.

Chapter 3

"I'm sure that's Bismarck on the right bank up ahead," Ki said to Jessie. "Even if it's been a very long time since I was here, I still remember that much about coming here with Alex."

"It's grown to be a fairly sizable town," she replied, without taking her eyes off the sprawling cluster of buildings the *Josephine* was approaching. "I was just a little girl when Alex brought me here on one of the trips I took with him. But you ought to recall that trip, Ki. I'm sure you were with us, because you always traveled with Alex."

"Of course I do," Ki said. "Alex was in a hurry and we were here just long enough to rest a little while from the bumpy train ride we'd had. Bismarck was the end of the tracks for the Northern Pacific, and we were here for only an evening and a morning before we had to start back. If we hadn't gone on the boat, we'd have had to wait a week for the next train."

"I'll have to admit, I don't remember that much about it," Jessie confessed. "About all I'm sure of is that Bismarck didn't look the way it does now. There were only two or perhaps three brick buildings here then, unless my memory's wrong."

"No, I think you're right," Ki said. "I was here with Alex later, twice, I believe. Each time we came back, the town had gotten bigger, and there were more brick buildings that had replaced the old wooden ones."

"But I don't even remember that there was anything on the west side of the river," Jessie went on, turning her gaze on the stream's western bank. "Now it looks like a new town's grown up there."

"It's not a town, Jessie. It's an army post."

"Of course! In a real town like Bismarck the buildings are all different. On an army post they all look alike."

Before Ki could speak, Joe Foreman's voice sounded behind them. He said, "I was just wishing Fort Lincoln had a different name. As a matter of fact, I was wishing it was called Fort Berthold."

"Now, why would you wish a thing like that?" Jessie asked.

"Because I'm billeted to Fort Berthold. It's another fifty miles or so farther upstream," Foreman said with a smile. "And you've told me that you and Ki will be getting off here at Bismarck."

"You're not even stopping off here, to report or something like that?" Jessie asked.

Foreman shook his head. "No. I heard some barracks gossip before I left. After Custer made a jackass of himself and gave the army a bad name at Little Bighorn, the brass hats made up their minds not to give the redskins another chance like that. We're asking them to be nice little boys and surrender."

"And are they?" Ki asked.

"Not so's you'd notice." Foreman replied. "I don't

know how much of what's been happening has trickled back to Texas, but Crazy Horse was killed sorta accidental-like after he'd said he was ready to surrender. Right after that, Little Horse and Crow King surrendered, so that eased things up a bit."

"Wasn't Crazy Horse their main chief?" Ki asked.

"One of them," Foreman said. "But there's plenty left. The redskins have a lot of chiefs. Some of 'em came in after the first three surrendered. Little Horse has given up and so has Crow King. That's not good enough, though."

"Do you think the others are going to surrender?" Jessie frowned. "Or will there be more fighting?"

"It's hard to say, Jessie, and I wouldn't try to guess," Foreman answered. "Ever since Custer got whipped so bad, some of the brass hats have been worried. They think the redskins might start attacking towns, now that they've shown they can win such a big fight against the army."

"So the army's waiting to show the Indians they're wrong?" Ki asked.

"Not exactly, Ki," Foreman said. "We're just waiting and watching right now. But there are still plenty of Indians to keep an eye on, you know. Sitting Bull and Gall and Rain-in-the-Face and White Eagle made a clean getaway with their fighting men. We can't touch them right now because they got across the border into Canada."

"And you can't cross the border?" Ki asked.

Foreman shrugged as he went on, "Not without Canada saying we can, which they sure haven't done so far."

"Does that mean those chiefs you just mentioned are going to go free?" Jessie frowned.

"Well, they're still free now. And they're the smartest of the big chiefs left. Not only that, they've got more'n enough fighting men between 'em to give our soldiers a real bad time and do a lot more mischief."

"What you're saying is that the army's ready to fight." Ki put in.

"Sure," Foreman said. "That's what us soldiers are for. But you won't hear any of us bellyaching if the redskins decide to surrender."

By this time the *Josephine* had passed the first outlying houses of Bismarck and was changing course, its prow pointing at a gentle slant toward the shore. Men were already gathering at the streamside close to the docks and sheds that marked the landing. The vessel's whistle tooted another trill of short blasts.

For a small town in an isolated section of sparsely settled Dakota Territory, when it was observed from the river Bismarck looked less like a Western frontier town than it did like one of the small cities east of the Mississippi. It's streets began at the edge of the low bluff just behind the steamboat landing, where three long angular wharves broke the low-rising riverbank.

On the flat prairie above the rise the town's buildings and houses stretched along the stream in neat squares for a mile or more. The town itself formed a long narrow triangle with the river as its base. Its apex was a half-mile inland. Within the triangle, streets cut the town into squares. Most of the squares nearest the river were lined solidly with stores and business buildings, then the houses began.

A surprising number of the buildings in the town's business center were of cut stone or brick, some of them imposing blocks two and three stories high. Between the taller structures were less imposing frame buildings housing stores and shops.

"It's a bigger town than I remembered" Jessie remarked as the boat neared the bank and the buildings began to be hidden by the rise in the shoreline.

"Yes, it surprised me, too," Ki agreed. "But suppose I go get our luggage now. Then we'll be ready to step ashore as soon as the ship ties up."

Jessie acknowledged his offer with a nod and a smile and turned back to face Foreman. "I'd enjoy having more nights with you, Joe, but it looks like we'll have to say good-bye."

"That's just good-bye for now, Jessie," Foreman replied. He stepped up to her and took her in his arms. Their lips met and pressed in a long clinging kiss. Foreman would have held their embrace longer, but Jessie pushed him away very gently.

"We've said good-bye," she told him. "And even if it is just for now, I've got to get ready to step off when the ship ties up. But we've met again by chance, so maybe we'll meet another time the same way."

"I hope it'll be soon," Foreman told her. "Except that I know it won't be likely. As long as the redskins are cutting up in these parts, there's not much chance of me getting back to Texas."

"Likely or not, I've got to get over to the land side of the ship," Jessie said. Her voice was firmer now. "And here comes Ki with our luggage. Good-bye, Joe. It was wonderful being with you again, even for a short time."

Evading Foreman's efforts to embrace her again, Jessie slipped away and moved quickly to join Ki, who had started across the crowded strip of deck. The riverboat had tied up at the dock while Jessie and Fore-

31

man were saying their good-byes. Ki was standing a bit away from the side of the ship, watching one of the vessel's hands, who was removing a section of the rail. On the deck beside the man the short gangplank lay ready to be pushed across the gap between ship and pier.

"What sort of plan have you made for us to follow here in Bismarck, Jessie?" Ki asked as she stopped beside him.

"No real plan," she said. "I didn't answer that odd letter this Pendergast wrote and didn't send word to Bob Stevens that we were coming here."

"That'll give us time to look around quietly and form our own ideas about what's going on," Ki said.

"Exactly. I'll want to stop at the bank before I talk to Bob. Bankers know just about everything that's going on in a town this size. But the first thing I want to do is check into a hotel and bathe and even rest an hour or two."

"When you say hotel, I suppose you mean the Merchants'? As I recall, that's the one where we stayed when we were here with Alex."

"It's old, but I suppose it's still the most comfortable hotel in town. Of course, there've probably been some new ones built since the last time I was here, but I'd still rather stay at the one I remember," Jessie said.

"That's where we'll head, then," Ki agreed. "It's just a little ways from here."

"If those bags aren't too big a burden, I'd as soon walk to the hotel. Or perhaps there's a livery rig that we can hire to take us and our luggage to the hotel."

"They're no real burden," Ki assured her as they crossed the gangplank and stepped ashore.

A gentle slope with a well-worn trail led up from

the bank of the river. As they reached the top, a man called, "Hackney over here, folks! You got a pretty good load to lug, and it won't cost only fifty cents for me to haul both of you and your bags into town and put you down right where you're headed for!"

"We'll ride," Jessie decided. "I'd like to get a quick look at the town, anyhow."

Though neither Jessie nor Ki were strangers to frontier communities, Bismarck did not fit into the mould of any they'd seen before. Almost half the buildings along the streets of the business section were of brick or stone, and many of the latter rose two stories, a few three stories, to tower above the less-imposing structures.

"At least we'll be able to go directly to the bank instead of floundering around," Jessie remarked. "There it is now."

"And another bank right across the street from it," Ki told her as he pointed. "Both of them look prosperous, too."

"I'd say the whole town looks prosperous, Ki," Jessie said. "This certainly is different from the struggling little frontier place that I remember."

By this time the hackman was reining up in front of the cut-stone facade of the hotel. Ki jumped out and lifted their bags from the vehicle before offering his hand to Jessie as she alighted.

"I'm sure you'll want to rest a while before you talk to Bob Stevens, or start finding out about this Pendergast fellow?" he asked as they went inside.

"I want a bath more than anything else," Jessie replied. "Then we can look around town and get our bearings. Besides getting an idea of what Bismarck's like, I want to stop in at the bank that carries our accounts here. After that, we'll really settle down to business."

"Miss Starbuck," the banker said as he bowed. "I'm very delighted to meet you at last, though I feel that I've known you for many years. But I don't suppose you'd recall having come to our bank with your father quite some time ago."

"I'm afraid I don't, Mr. Davis," Jessie replied. She gestured toward Ki, who'd stopped a short distance away. "You'd probably be more likely to remember Ki than you would me."

"Yes, of course. Ki." Davis nodded. The banker was a short fat man. His eyes bulged between little pillows of eyelids, and he had a puffy double chin that wabbled as he moved his head. He went on, "Ki was perhaps the first Oriental to visit Bismarck, when your father brought him here."

Davis faced Ki for the first time but did not offer to shake hands as he said, "You might be interested in knowing that we now have quite a group of them. If you'd like to visit your countrymen while you're here, they've settled in a—well, a neighborhood, I suppose, at the north end of Fifth Street."

"If I have time, I'll probably stroll down there for a look around," Ki told the banker. "But that will depend on how long Jessie stays and how busy we are."

"I hope it's not trouble that's brought you here, Miss Starbuck," Davis said with a frown, turning back to Jessie.

"If any of the Starbuck properties here is having trouble, I'm not aware of it," Jessie told the banker. "But I don't have the opportunity to visit them as often as I like. Dakota Territory's a bit out of the way,

34

when I start from my ranch down in Texas."

"Well, now that you're finally visiting Bismarck again, Miss Starbuck, how can I be of service to you?" Davis asked. "If you'd prefer to talk privately, we can go into my office where we won't be disturbed."

"Perhaps that would be better," Jessie agreed. "Ki and I"—she stressed Ki's name very slightly—"haven't only come to look at the Starbuck holdings here. I wanted to find out a bit more about this part of the country and its future."

Davis led the way into his office and pulled chairs up to his wide polished desk before settling into a chair himself. Before the banker could speak, Jessie took the initiative.

"I suppose that if there was any sort of trouble developing at the Starbuck mine—or the riverboats and shipyard, for that matter—you'd be among the first to hear of it," she said.

Davis nodded. "I'm sure I would be informed."

"Then perhaps you can tell me what these men who call themselves the Friends of the Working Man might do to the Starbuck mines or the shipyard," Jessie suggested.

For a moment the banker sat silently, then he asked, "Are they threatening your help here, Miss Starbuck?"

"I'm sorry that I don't have any details to give you," Jessie said. "But Bob Stevens—I'm sure you know him, the manager of the Starbuck properties here—mentioned them in one of his recent reports," Jessie said. "I got the impression they're becoming very active in Bismarck. What can you tell us about them?"

"Very little, I'm afraid," Davis replied. "They're a very secretive group. Troublemakers, of course."

"Just how much trouble are they making?" Ki asked when Jessie did not continue her questioning.

"I haven't heard of any real trouble yet," the banker said. "I'm aware that there've been some threats made by the outfit, threats to the miners who don't want to have anything to do with them. I understand there've been fights in a few of the saloons when they try to enlist miners who've refused to join them."

"What about property damage?" Jessie asked. "Have these Friends of the Working Man been acting here the way I've heard of them behaving in other places?"

Shaking his head, the banker answered, "If there's been any sort of violence or vandalism, I haven't heard about it."

"Perhaps there's been some that was never reported," Ki suggested.

"That's possible, of course," the banker agreed.

"Others seem to've heard of trouble," Jessie put in. "From his letter, this Mr. Pendergast is one of them. And now that I've brought up his name, perhaps you'll tell me a little bit about him."

Davis was silent for a moment, then he said, "I'm afraid there isn't anyone in Bismarck who knows a great deal about Mr. Pendergast, Miss Starbuck."

"He's secretive, then?" Jessie frowned.

"Perhaps I'd better say that's he's completely silent about his affairs," the banker answered. "Pendergast didn't choose to place his account in this bank or the other one just down the street. He's been here something like two or three years now, but he still banks in Chicago."

"Mr. Davis," Jessie said, "I've had a chance to look at banks from the inside, largely due to the bank

36

stocks that I inherited from my father. I'm quite well aware of the information bankers have on people who're potentially large depositors."

Though the banker's expression did not change, he blinked his eyes several times before replying, "Of course, when Pendergast writes a check—which isn't often—to pay for a purchase at one of the local stores which carries its account with us, we have to forward it to his bank in Chicago for clearance."

"And I'm sure you keep records of some sort for your private information, in case Pendergast should decide to become one of your bank's depositors," Jessie suggested.

Jessie's question had caught the banker off-guard. He began blinking his eyes again as the realization dawned on him that she was very well-informed indeed about the inner working of banks and the habits of bankers. At last he cleared his throat and replied.

"Confidential memorandums, Miss Starbuck," he said. "For bank use only, of course."

"Of course," Jessie agreed. She stood up. "I wouldn't think of asking you to share your confidential memorandums with me." She turned to Ki and went on: "We've taken up too much of Mr. Davis's time, Ki. I'm sure there are things that need his attention, and we have other matters to attend to ourselves."

"Now, I'm not all that pressed for time, Miss Starbuck!" the banker protested. "Since this is your first visit—"

"But not my last," Jessie said. Her voice was cold. "I'll find time to drop in at least once more, Mr. Davis, but for the moment I'll say good day and leave you to your work."

As they left the bank, Ki turned to Jessie and said,

"You certainly left no doubts with Davis that refusing to tell you more about this fellow Pendergast didn't exactly please you."

"That's what I intended to do," Jessie replied. "And now we'll just underline things for him."

"How do you plan—"

"Very simply, Ki. We'll walk across the street and go into that other bank," she said. "I'm sure Davis is watching us right now, and I'm equally sure that we can find a reason for asking that bank we're heading for to let us go out their back door."

Ki was smiling broadly even before Jessie had finished her explanation. He said, "And after Mr. Davis worries a while when he's watched long enough, he's not likely to waste any time in sending you his confidential file on Pendergast."

"Exactly. We don't have to do anything in a hurry, Ki. I don't like to go into a situation without enough ammunition. And I'm sure that by now Pendergast is wondering why I haven't given him an answer to his offer to buy the mine and the shipyard and the river fleet."

"So you intend to let him dangle for a while? You do intend to meet with him, though?"

"Of course," Jessie said, nodding. "But in my own good time, and only after I've found out quite a bit more about him."

They'd crossed the street and reached the door of the bank by now. Ki held the door open for Jessie, then followed her inside. They stood in the lobby for a moment, looking at the busy tellers on one side and the desks on the other, then Jessie started for one of the desks. The young man sitting behind it looked up at them.

"Can I help you with something?" he asked, his eyes shifting from Jessie to Ki, then back to her, a slight puzzled frown on his face.

"I—well, I know you'll think this is a strange request," Jessie replied. "I came in here to get off the street, to avoid being seen by someone—" She broke off and looked back over her shoulder, frowning, before going on: "I don't think he's followed us, but I was wondering if you can let us out by your back door?"

By the time Jessie had finished, the young man was smiling, though he was obviously trying to hide his amusement. He stood up as he said, "I'll certainly be happy to accommodate you, ma'am. I think I understand your situation. Just come with me."

Three or four minutes later Jessie and Ki were on their way back to the hotel.

Chapter 4

"How long do you think it'll be before you get some sort of reaction from your friendly banker?" Ki asked Jessie as they started toward the Merchants' Hotel after circling around the street on which the banks were located.

"Very soon, Ki. Davis's bank certainly looks prosperous, but even the biggest banks hate to lose customers."

"I see your point," Ki said, nodding. "Competition can be a very compelling thing when it's put to use."

"Exactly. I'm sure Mr. Davis will reconsider his refusal very soon."

They'd walked on in silence for a few steps when Ki said, "I've been thinking while we were going around corners, Jessie."

"And?" Jessie asked when he paused.

Ki replied, "Davis made a remark about there being quite a few Orientals in Bismarck now."

"And there weren't when you were here before, with Alex?"

"Just a half-dozen. Remember, Bismarck hadn't

been here but a short time when you father and I first came here."

"Then you know some of your countrymen from those visits?"

"Two or three, enough to open closed doors for me. Some of them probably work at the mine, and it's possible that our banker friend might hire some Oriental servants. Gossip is gossip wherever you go, Jessie, and having a few little scraps of inside information has helped us before."

"Of course," Jessie agreed. "And we'll need all the information we can get. I think it's a good idea."

"Then I'll go and have a look tonight. I haven't been here for a long time, so nobody's going to think it odd if I ask a lot of questions," Ki went on. "It might be a while before they talk freely until we get reacquainted, but they'll talk more freely tomorrow and the next night. Of course, if you have other plans—"

Jessie shook her head. "We'll be going to Bob Stevens's office at the mine later this afternoon, and I'll invite him to dinner at the hotel. That will leave you free to do all the calling on your countrymen that you care to."

"Speaking of dinner, there's one thing we seem to've overlooked today."

"Yes. Lunch," Jessie agreed. "I thought we might go on back to the hotel and have lunch sent up to my room. I suppose you're hungry enough to step across the hall and join me?"

"Don't have any doubts about that," Ki said. "Suddenly I'm so hungry that I don't even care what you order."

• • •

Jessie and Ki were just finishing their meal when someone tapped at the door. Ki rose to open it. A neatly uniformed bellboy holding a large thin envelope stood in the hall.

"This just come in at the desk downstairs," he said. "It's for Miss Jessica Starbuck."

"I'll take it and hand it to her," Ki told the youth. He dug into the folds of the sash that supported his loose trousers and brought out a coin, which he handed to the bellboy as he took the envelope. Closing the door, he took the envelope to Jessie. As he handed it to her, he said, "Since your banker is the only one who knows you're here, I'll make a guess."

"I'm sure your guess would be the same as mine," Jessie replied as she began opening the envelope. "It worked out just as I'd planned, Ki. Mr. Davis watched us going into the other bank and after he'd thought things over, he changed his mind about sharing whatever information he has on Elzey Pendergast's check-writing habits."

She took two long pages of blue-lined foolscap from the envelope. Pinned to them was a smaller sheet of imprinted bank stationery which bore a short message penned in bold copperplate script. While Ki listened, Jessie read the note aloud.

"My dear Miss Starbuck," it began. "After your departure, I reconsidered my somewhat hasty decision to keep from you certain matters about which you were curious, and have now decided that my refusal was an error.

"Whether the enclosed will be of any help to you is uncertain, but I will rely on your discretion not to reveal the contents of the attached pages. If by chance this should happen, I am sure that you will remain silent as to their source. Your obedient servant and so on."

"Well," Jessie commented as she unfolded the long sheets of the two pages enclosed. "It seems that Mr. Davis really had a change of heart after we'd left him and he had time to think about my request a second time. Let's see what we can deduce from the checks that this Mr. Pendergast has written."

Handing one of the pages to Ki, Jessie began scanning the second herself. The entries had been made in chronological order and were quite uniform: they consisted of a check number, a date, and the name of the payee, together with the amount for which the check had been written.

After her first quick glance at the page she held, Jessie decided that the logical approach was to begin with the last entry and work forward. She'd covered less than half the page before recognizing the name of a payee which had appeared near the bottom line, and a few lines farther up the page the same name appeared again.

In each case the check carrying the recurring name was made out in the amount of one thousand dollars. It was always sandwiched between a miscellany of perhaps a half-dozen small checks which had been written in payment for purchases at stores in Bismarck. Hurriedly, Jessie went through the remainder of the list. As she'd suspected, the name that had caught her attention showed up at intervals roughly four weeks apart.

"I'm not sure this means anything, Ki," she said. A small frown had formed on her face as she was going through the list, "But our Mr. Pendergast is paying a regular salary—or at least he's sending money regu-

43

larly—to someone in Chicago named Caroline Simmons."

With his forefinger, Ki indicated an entry on the sheet he'd been examining. He said, "I was just getting ready to ask you if you'd run into that name, Jessie. It's already shown up three times on this page I've been looking at."

"Of course, it could mean any one of several things," Jessie said with a thoughtful frown. "The check could've been sent to his clerk or secretary in Chicago, for salary and office expenses, though that's the least likely thing that comes to my mind. Of course, this Caroline Simmons could be a needy relative he's supporting, or a married daughter—or he might be keeping a mistress there."

"I hardly think she'd be a mistress," Ki said. "Bismarck doesn't have a reputation for being a straitlaced town, and Pendergast would simply have brought her here with him."

"Yes, that's true," Jessie agreed. "But there wasn't anything else that caught my attention."

Ki nodded, then said, "While we're still thinking of Pendergast, I've been getting curious about how you intend to reply to his offer."

"I'll refuse it, of course," Jessie replied promptly. "Even if the amount of business we're doing here now isn't great, Bismarck's growing fast, from the little we've seen of it. It's on the way to becoming a real city. Then the mine and the shipping properties will become very profitable."

Ki smiled. "I'm sure that's what Alex would've said, too. But it's getting late, Jessie. If we intend to go out to the mine today, we'd better start."

* * *

There were only two roads leading from Bismarck, one that ran parallel to the riverbank and another that led to the broad sweep of low hilly country east of the town. Ki was handling the reins of the nondescript mare that pulled the buggy Jessie had rented from the livery stables beyond the hotel, and he left them slack most of the time, letting the horse pick its own way over the rough road, rutted deeply from the passage of heavily laden coal wagons coming into town from the Starbuck mine.

They reached a sign, a board notched at one end and pointed at the other. The pointed end indicated a road narrower and more deeply rutted than the one over which they'd been traveling. The board bore the faintly visible words STARBUCK MINE, and Ki turned into it.

After they'd covered a quarter of a mile in the jouncing, swaying buggy, Jessie turned to him. "I'm finding this a very unpleasant surprise, Ki," she said frowning. "This road doesn't speak well of Bob Stevens's management. It's certainly no credit to a Starbuck property."

"I was thinking the same thing," Ki agreed. "And I have a pretty good idea of what you're going to tell him about it."

"That'll depend on what we find out after we talk to him. I keep wondering if the trouble up here doesn't run deeper than we think. Bob may have had too many problems to attend to keeping the road in good shape."

Ahead of them, coming around one of the road's many curves, two heavily laden wagons appeared. They were swaying and jolting on the rutted surface, heading for the river. Ki turned out onto the grassed prairie before the wagons reached the buggy. Neither of the teamsters appeared to notice Jessie and Ki. They sat humped in their seats, watching the road, and did not wave or even nod as they passed.

"I wouldn't call the people up here especially friendly," Jessie remarked as Ki sawed the reins to turn the horse back onto the ruts again.

"Maybe we're just too far north," Ki said. "Or maybe they have something more important on their minds than the coal they're hauling."

"That's what I've begun wondering about, Ki," Jessie said, nodding. "I'm beginning to think that whatever's going on here just might be even more serious than we'd anticipated."

"Don't you think that Bob Stevens would've written you if there's something wrong?"

"He should have, of course." Jessie frowned. "But perhaps it began as just a minor problem he could take care of himself. Then after it began to grow, he hesitated to tell me the full story, because that'd be admitting that he made a bad mistake."

"We'll find out very soon," Ki said, pointing to the array of buildings that had just appeared ahead as they reached the end of a long gentle curve in the road. "There's the mine, just ahead of us."

Jessie studied the scene in front of them. The mine was not at all as she remembered it from that long-ago visit with Alex. Then, it had consisted only of an engine house and a small shack that served as an office. Now in addition to the engine house, which had changed little since she'd seen it years ago, there were three huge barns to provide shelter for the horses and wagons during the cold snowy winters, as well as a long window-studded bunkhouse. The old office shack had been replaced by a large two-story building.

Only a few men were in the area around the buildings. They were in scattered groups, most of them near the bunkhouse, but a few stood in bunches of three or four close to the office or stables. The barren ground around the engine house was covered with cone-shaped stacks of coal. Two wagons were visible at the edge of the coal stacks, and men were shoveling coal into them. Closer at hand, the area around the engine house structure itself, with a tall windlass rising like a misshapen spire from its center, was deserted.

"I'd never have recognized this place as the one I visited with Alex when he first started to develop it," Jessie admitted.

"It's changed, all right," Ki agreed. "Just as Bismarck has. This is growing country, and the mine's grown with it."

As Ki spoke, he was reining up at the hitching rail that stretched in front of the office building. He leaped out and turned to give his hand to Jessie when she alighted. Before they could start away from the buggy, the office door opened and an old-young man came out.

When Ki got his first clear view of the newcomer, he turned to Jessie and said in a half-whisper, "That's Bob Stevens, but I didn't recognize him for a moment. It's only been a few years since I saw him last, when I was here with Alex, but he's aged twenty years!"

"I'm glad you told me," Jessie said. "I've only seen him once before, and I didn't recognize him."

By this time Stevens was within speaking distance of them. He stepped around the high buggy wheels and stopped in front of Jessie and Ki.

"Miss Starbuck!" he exclaimed. "You're the last

person in the world I'd have expected to see! It's been such a long time since your visit here with your father that I didn't recognize you at first glance!"

"That was quite a while ago," Jessie agreed. She indicated their surroundings with a wave of her hand as she went on: "And things have changed quite a lot. I can just glance around and see that the mine's grown quite substantially."

"Your father was very shrewd," Stevens said. "He knew how to pick places that would grow. Dakota Territory's building up fast, Bismarck's growing with it." Turning to Ki, he went on: "Even though you and Mr. Starbuck were here once since Miss Starbuck's last visit, you've surely noticed the difference."

"Of course," Ki said, nodding. "But even since I was here last, the mine's grown a lot." He flicked his eyes toward Jessie and caught hers as he went on: "I'm sure Miss Starbuck would like to get a fairly thorough look at the mine while she's here, though this might not be the best time."

"No, it isn't," Jessie agreed.

Though she followed Ki's hint, Jessie was puzzled as to its meaning for a moment. Then she realized that Ki's intention was to gain time for them to carry out the investigation they'd discussed on their way to the mine.

Turning back to Stevens, she said, "But I'd want to put on some more suitable clothes and some heavy shoes before I go into the mine, and I also think you and I should visit for a while first. The main reason that I came out here is to ask if you're free to have dinner with me this evening. It will give us a chance to talk without taking your attention off things that I'm sure you must need to be doing now."

48

"Why—of course," Stevens replied. "I don't go into Bismarck every day, but I'd certainly enjoy dining with you."

"Suppose you just show us around for a few minutes while we're here now," Jessie suggested. "Then we'll meet and talk about the mine this evening."

"There's not much to see above ground," Stevens said. "I'm sure you know that your father bought a substantial spread of land, primarily to preserve the mineral rights."

Jessie nodded. "Something like twenty square miles, if I remember correctly. And he also bought some waterfront acreage for the shipyard and land around the wharves for the riverboats."

"Yes. If you plan to go and look at them today, I'll be very glad to go with you," Stevens told her.

"We'll put that off until later," Jessie answered. "And I don't expect there's much else that I can see here without going down into the mine."

"Not a great deal," Stevens agreed.

"All that I really came out here for was to invite you to dinner," Jessie went on. "Now that we've settled that, Ki and I will go on back to town. We may drive along the river for a quick look at the shipyard, but there's no need for you to go with us. We won't stop there; all I'm interested in is getting an idea of things. We can go there for a more thorough look after our chat this evening."

Stevens nodded. "You're stopping at the Merchants' Hotel, I suppose?" he asked.

Jessie nodded. "Yes. I'll expect you about seven, and we'll have a long visit about the mine and the shipyard and the riverboats."

• • •

As she and Ki were jolting in the seat of the buggy over the rough road back to Bismarck, Jessie turned to him and said, "You know Bob Stevens a bit better than I do, Ki. Am I mistaken, or did he seem to be a little uneasy when he first saw us?"

"He was surprised, but that's only to be expected," Ki answered. "Of course, he didn't have any advance notice of your visit, and just seeing you here must have startled him a bit."

"If his position and mine were reversed, I'm sure I'd've been startled, too," Jessie agreed. "Now, let me see if I can remember where the shipyard is."

"It's just beyond the point where the river road forks to the mine," Ki said. "We turn upstream, and then the shipyard's only a mile or so from the fork."

"I don't intend to do more than look at the shipyard, Ki," Jessie told him. "I'm really just getting oriented here."

"We're not pressed for time, if you want to stop and get a close look."

Jessie shook her head. "I don't know enough about shipbuilding to understand what the men there would be doing. All I want to see is how it's laid out and what they're working at, so I won't be at sea when I talk with Bob Stevens this evening."

After they reached the turnoff, the road was a bit less rough and bumpy. A short ride brought them within sight of the two tall masts that towered above the rise in the riverbank on a broad shelving stretch of land that ran back from the edge of the river.

As they got closer, they heard the thunking of mallets, and then they could see the hulls of two small ships resting on the intricate frameworks of supporting timbers. A dozen or so men swarmed over the smaller

50

of the half-completed vessels, stepping one of its masts into place. Jessie reined in.

"It's a busy place, isn't it?" she asked.

"It certainly seems to be," Ki agreed. "Of course, with the trouble we've heard the railroad's having, I'm sure there's a need for the kind of small riverboats the yard turns out."

They sat watching for a few moments, then Jessie nodded and said, "I'm satisfied, now that I've seen the shipyard, Ki. At least I can talk a bit more easily with Stevens. That's the only reason I wanted to look."

She wheeled the buggy around and slapped the reins over the horse's back. The road ran close to the riverbank here, and as they drew closer to Bismarck they could see two small river steamers and a solid line of barges at the landing ahead. In addition, a trio of flatboats were crossing the stream, their course slanting downriver, heading for the landing that served the fort on the opposite bank of the wide Missouri.

"I feel better about things now, Ki," Jessie remarked as she reined the buggy onto the street that ended abruptly at the high levee which stood between the river and the small residences which dotted the ground between the river and the town. "Not having visited here for such a long time, I had no idea what to expect."

"Oh, it's growing into a city very fast," Ki agreed. "And quite likely will keep growing for years ahead."

Jessie nodded. She was gazing ahead, turning to look along the intersecting streets, searching for the hotel. She saw its white bulk at the third or fourth intersection and reined the buggy into it. As she tightened the reins to halt the horse, Ki suggested, "Why don't you get out here and let me take the buggy around the corner to the livery, Jessie? You don't intend to go anywhere else today, do you?"

"Of course not," Jessie replied. She looped the reins around the buggywhip and started to step to the sidewalk as she went on: "I'm going to enjoy not having anything to do except think about the questions I intend to ask Bob Stevens this evening. I've a few things to discuss with him in addition to the mine's operation."

"And while you're having dinner, I'll be in the Oriental neighborhood, looking for information," Ki said. "I'll be back as soon as I wheel the buggy around to the livery, so just tap on my door if you want me for anything."

Jessie went into the hotel and climbed the stairs to the second floor. The wide door-lined corridor was empty. She took the key to her room from her pocket as she walked along the hallway and let herself in.

While she and Ki had been out, the hotel's chambermaids had been busy. Her bed had been remade, her few toilet articles had been rearranged neatly on the chiffonier, and the door of the wardrobe beyond it had been closed.

As she glanced around the room, Jessie saw only one thing that was at odds with its neatness. At the broad double window that broke one wall of the spacious chamber, one of the heavy draped curtains that hung at each side of the gauzy center netting was wrinkled and awry instead of falling in the neat folds its companion showed in its sweep from the top of the window to the carpet. More by habit than anything else, Jessie stepped to the window and lifted the curtain to shake out its creases. As she bent to straighten a stubbornly crinkled spot, she glanced down at the carpeted floor and froze.

Four sticks of dynamite had been hidden by the heavy drapery. The fuse from the explosive cylinders ran up the wall behind the narrow end drapery to the bottom of the windowsill and disappeared under the sash.

Chapter 5

For a moment Jessie stood staring at the four long round explosive sticks. The dynamite had been lashed together with wrappings of stout cord at each end, and she could see the glint of a copper cap shining at the point where the fuse had been inserted into one of the sticks.

Jessie was no stranger to dynamite. She'd seen it used on many occasions at one or another of the Starbuck mines, as well as in North Coast timbering operations, where lumberjacks used it to blast logjams free. She knew that the red paper-covered sticks were harmless until a spark from the fuse reached the copper cap imbedded in one of the cylinders. She was also well aware that even a small bump might jar the fulminite-filled cap to set off the stick of dynamite into which it was embedded, and that the explosion of that stick would detonate the others almost instantaneously.

Moving very carefully, Jessie let the curtain drop and began backing away from the window. She'd taken only two short steps when a gentle tapping sounded at the door. Jessie recognized the rhythmic pattern of the soft knocks. She made her next backward step longer than those she'd been taking, then twirled and hurried to the door.

Certain that her visitor was the one she wanted above all others to see, she opened the door. Ki stood in the open doorway, his hand coming up to knock again.

"Ki!" Jessie exclaimed hurriedly. "I was just starting across the hall to see if you'd come in yet, so that I could warn you!"

"Warn me of what?" Ki asked.

He took a half-step, starting into the room, but Jessie pressed her hand to his chest and said, "No! Don't come in! This room might explode any minute!"

After sharing so many tense moments with her during their long fight against the cartel, Ki knew quite well that Jessie would never joke about such an important matter. In spite of her warning he gently moved her hand aside and came into the room.

"How?" he asked.

"Dynamite. Four sticks lashed together," she said tersely. "One of them is fused and ready."

"Where?"

Jessie indicated the window. "Under the drapery at the left side of the big window. The fuse runs out the window."

"Stand right where you are," Ki said over his shoulder as he started toward the window. As he moved he took a *shuriken* from the sheath strapped to his forearm.

Reaching the window, Ki carefully lifted the bottom of the drape and bent forward to examine the explosive. For a moment he studied the four menacing red cylinders, then he locked the *shuriken* between his

55

thumb and forefingers and with the razor-sharp edge of one of the throwing-blade's points he carefully severed the fuse at the place where it ran across the windowsill.

Over his shoulder he said to Jessie, "There won't be any explosion now."

As Jessie started to join him, he shook his head as he waved her back. She stopped halfway between the door and the window. Ki was still holding up the end of the drapery as he bent his head sidewise and peered through the filmy gauze netting that spanned the window between its draped sides.

"This window overlooks the alley in the back of the hotel," he said over his shoulder to Jessie. "The only thing you can see from it are the backs of the buildings that face the next street. There's no one in the alley, as far as I can tell. About all I can see is that the fuse is draped over the outside windowsill and hangs down into the alley."

"But now that you've cut it away from the dynamite, the fuse doesn't mean anything," Jessie said. "It's harmless."

"Of course," he agreed. "But I'd hoped to get a glimpse of someone lurking down there waiting to light it."

"I doubt that whoever set this trap would still be around," Jessie said. Her voice was as level and calm as though she and Ki were commenting on the weather or the time of day. "Whoever put that dynamite here will more than likely come back tonight. I'm sure they were planning to set the charge off after I'd come in and gone to bed."

"I'd say you're right," Ki agreed. "But let me finish this job before we start trying to figure out who might've planted this dynamite bomb and why they wanted to blow you up."

Hunkering down beside the window, Ki again used the sharp edge of one of the *shuriken*'s needle-sharp points to cut through the heavy cords that bound the dynamite sticks into a bundle. He worked very slowly and carefully as he separated the fused sticks from the others. Then, using another point-tip, he skillfully cut a shallow circle around the tiny shoulder that had been crimped into the rim of the copper cap. Finally he laid the blade on the floor and grasped the shoulder of the cap to twist it gently until he could lift it out of the dynamite stick.

Ki laid the stub of fuse and the cap which was still connected to it on the windowsill. With the now-harmless stick of dynamite still in his hand, he turned at last to face Jessie.

"If you've been holding your breath, as I have, you can let go of it," he told her. "There's really nothing for us to worry about now."

"Yes, I know that much about dynamite," Jessie said. "I remember one of the lumberjacks at one of our timber stands up on the North Coast explaining to me that if dynamite hasn't gotten old and unstable, it won't explode without a cap to set it off, unless it has a spark or sharp blow to trigger it."

"From the way these dynamite sticks look, they're new and fresh," Ki said.

"In that case, it probably came from a store here in Bismarck, and we might be able to find out something about the man who bought it," Jessie suggested as she closed the door and came to stand beside Ki. "And there's the fuse, too. It looks as new as the dynamite. Perhaps they came from the same place."

"You're probably right," Ki said. "But that will have to wait." He pulled aside the gauzy curtain and pushed his face to the glass, trying to get a better look down into the alley. Shaking his head, he turned away from the window. "There's no one down there that I can see, and I don't want to draw any attention to this window by opening it and leaning out."

"You think somebody might be watching the window?"

"It's possible, but it's more likely that whoever set the charge moved away as soon as they finished."

"They wouldn't've had any trouble getting a key," Jessie said. "Or even getting into the room without one. All they'd have to do was tell the chambermaids this was their room and they'd forgotten to get a key at the desk when they came in."

Ki shook his head as he said, "That'd be too risky— the chambermaid would remember them. My guess is that they walked through the lobby without anyone paying attention to them, came up here, and opened your door with a skeleton key. They set the charge, coiled the fuse up and laid it on the windowsill with a long cord attached to the end. They'd have prepared the dynamite and fuse in advance, of course."

"Of course," Jessie agreed. "Putting the dynamite in place and dropping the cord out of the window wouldn't've taken long. And people don't really look at one another when they're going through hotel lobbies."

Ki went on: "After they got out of the hotel, they'd just have to walk to the corner and turn down the alley. They pulled the string to get the end of the fuse, coiled it up so that it'd be above the heads of anyone

58

going through the alley, and then got away fast. I doubt that anyone noticed them."

"Of course not," Jessie said, nodding. "The whole job could've been finished in five or ten minutes."

Ki dropped the drape and smoothed it and the gauzy curtain before turning back to Jessie and going on: "Looking at the fuse at this end isn't going to help us a great deal. I didn't lean out to look because someone might've been watching in the alley, but I'm positive that when we get downstairs we'll find it's been looped up above eye level and is dangling against the wall."

"Where someone passing through the alley wouldn't be likely to notice it," Jessie agreed. "Then whoever put the dynamite in here planned to come back tonight and wait until they were sure I was in the room before they lighted the fuse."

"I'd say you've hit the nail on the head," Ki told her. "The important thing now is to think of somebody who'd want you dead."

As she stepped to the nearest chair and sat down, Jessie said, "That's the first question that popped into my mind when I saw the bomb."

"And I'm sure your first thought must've been about the same as mine," Ki agreed. "Someone who survived when we smashed the cartel."

"Yes, I did think that for a moment. And there's a chance our suspicions are right. It might be some survivor, someone who's trying to bring the cartel back to life."

"That was the rest of my thought," Ki said. "Bismarck would be isolated enough to serve one of them very well as a place to go to cover."

"They certainly wouldn't have to worry about someone running into them here who'd recognize their connection with that ugly group," Jessie went on thoughtfully.

"No. And aside from the hotel and the bank, and our visit to the coal mine and shipyard, we haven't been outside the hotel. Except for the men at the Circle Star and the mysterious Elzey Pendergast, there's no one who'd know we're here."

"If this Pendergast knows it, Arthur Davis at the bank must have told him," Jessie said with a frown.

"Don't overlook the men at the shipyard," Ki cautioned her. "We may have been seen by some of them."

Jessie shook her head as she replied, "No, Ki. I somehow can't see one of the cartel's important members working as a shipwright."

"That leaves the banks, then," Ki said thoughtfully.

Jessie nodded agreement as she said, "Yes. Either Davis's or the one we went through to give him something to think about."

"One's as good a possibility as the other," Ki agreed.

"We certainly can't afford to overlook either of them," Jessie went on. "But even without having seen him, I'd say that this Elzey Pendergast seems more likely. I don't suppose we'll get any sort of clue from the dynamite or the fuse."

Ki shook his head. "In a town like Bismarck, right on the frontier, there must be at least a dozen places where dynamite and fuse and caps are kept in stock. It'd be time wasted trying to find out who'd bought any recently."

"Then suppose we just go about our business," Jessie suggested. "Say nothing to anyone about this attempt to blow me to bits, and force whoever tried to to make another move."

"I think that's the best solution," Ki agreed. "And in the meantime, there's still that piece of fuse hanging from the window, and somebody will show up tonight to light it."

"You'll be watching in the alley, of course?"

"Certainly. But I'm not expecting anything to happen until the dynamiter's sure you're in your room. Even then, he might wait until the town's asleep."

A thoughtful frown had formed on Jessie's face while she and Ki talked. Now she said, "Bob Stevens is coming to the hotel to have dinner with me, and you were planning to go down to the Oriental district and listen to gossip. If you're going to watch the alley, I suppose you'll have to give up your plan, but I'll go ahead with mine."

Ki shook his head. "Our would-be dynamiter's not going to light his fuse until there's a light showing in the window of your room, Jessie. I'll still go down to Chinatown, because I've got to break the ice there and find somebody who can give me the answers to a few questions before I can do any real good. It'd be a mistake for me to seem too inquisitive on my first visit."

"Then what we need to do is to agree on our timing," Jessie said. "I can stretch out my dinner with Bob Stevens by asking a lot of questions—which I'd planned to do anyhow—and if it's necessary, I can just wait in the lobby until the time we set for me to go to my room."

"That's probably the best thing to do," Ki agreed. "Ten o'clock's about the high tide of activity in any Oriental district I've ever encountered. Suppose we set ten-thirty as the earliest time for you to light the lamp in your room."

"It won't be hard to keep Bob at the table until then," Jessie told Ki. "During dinner, I'll simply talk about anything except our operations here in Bismarck. After dinner, I'll start asking him about the mine and shipyard and shipping line, and I already have enough questions to ask about them to stretch out our after-dinner chat until ten-thirty."

"If you're a bit late getting to your room, it won't matter," Ki agreed. "I'll be in place by then. Just don't light the lamp in your room any earlier."

"Don't worry. You know that when I travel I always carry the little watch Alex got me from Mr. Tiffany's nice jewelry store. I'll pin it on and be in my room at exactly ten-thirty."

"Let's leave it at that, then. I'll be in the alley by ten-thirty, perhaps a bit earlier. Now, since we probably have a long night ahead of us, it might be a good idea to rest a while."

Jessie was keeping her promise to Ki. During her meal with Bob Stevens she chatted about the Circle Star, Sun, the size of Texas being almost twice that of Dakota Territory, her visits to some of the other Starbuck holdings, and any other topic that came to mind. Each time Stevens tried to switch her to talking about the properties for which he was responsible, she'd either change the subject quickly or ignore his efforts to bring up the mine, the shipyard, or the river freighters.

From time to time she glanced down at the small gold-cased watch pinned to the bosom of her dinner dress. After dessert had been served and their coffee cups refilled, she looked at the dial once more and saw that the time had come for her to start asking Stevens about the local Starbuck properties.

"Now that we can talk without interrupting our dinner, suppose we begin talking about the coal mine," she suggested. "That's what we're here for."

"I'm as ready as I'll ever be," Stevens replied.

Jessie began, "I was a bit surprised to see that in your last report you'd included financial statements for my operations here in Bismarck. I don't usually expect them until you've closed your books for the year. Did you have some special reason for sending them?"

Jessie saw at once that her sudden switch of topics had caught Stevens off-guard. He hesitated for a moment before he replied, "I didn't really intend them for you, Jessie. I keep that running tally of operations as a sort of running memorandum for my own use. My clerk is new on the job, and he included it by mistake in that report I sent you."

"I see," Jessie said. "As it happens, I was glad to get the figures. The shipyard is doing well, and so are the river freight boats. But I had no idea that production at the mine had fallen off so sharply. Are the ore veins petering out?"

Stevens made no reply for a moment and Jessie could see that he was either thinking hard about his answer or was trying to recall words that he'd framed earlier.

At last he said, "That's just a temporary matter. The fact is, we've been having trouble with a gang of labor agitators."

"They've slowed your work up, then?"

"A little. I keep trying to keep it up, of course."

"I'm sure you've found out who the agitators are?"

"They call themselves the Friends of the Working

63

Man, Jessie. I've heard they have their main head-quarters either in St. Louis or Chicago. I don't know a great deal about them, because they have some sort of oath of secrecy that they take."

"How long has this been going on, Bob?"

"Quite a while," Stevens admitted reluctantly.

"Why didn't you write me about this?" Jessie asked. "Or better still, you could've sent me a telegram."

"Well, I guess I figured wrong, but I kept telling myself they'd quit making trouble when they saw they weren't getting anywhere."

Jessie frowned. "What kind of trouble are they making?"

"Well, they started by trying to scare off our under-ground men, threatening to beat them up or even kill them if they didn't join this Friends outfit. Then they jumped some of our wagons and dumped the coal on the ground. The latest thing they've done is to find some way to get into the mine during the night, when we work short gangs. What they've done is weaken the safety columns in the main tunnels by undercutting them."

"But that could cause those tunnels to collapse!" Jessie exclaimed. "Our men could be killed!"

Stevens nodded. "I realize that, Jessie. Don't worry, all the safety columns have been reinforced now."

"Which doesn't mean they can't be weakened again, or even smashed to pieces," Jessie pointed out.

"Yes, of course. Luckily, nothing like that has hap-pened, and I know how serious it could be if they broke the columns all the way through. As soon as I can find trustworthy men, I'm going to set up guards and tell them to shoot if they have to."

"I suppose you've lost some of your best men because of the threats and the possibility of danger?" Jessie asked.

"A few. Some started leaving when these Friends of the Working Man began jumping them. At first they looked for the ones they were after in the saloons downtown here, but I hear that now they're even going to the homes of the men who refuse to listen to them, and beating them up."

"I don't suppose the miners like the idea of having two bosses instead of one?"

"Oh, a few are in favor of joining the Friends of the Working Man, but most of them had rather be left alone to earn their pay in peace."

"And what are these Friends of the Working Man after? Higher pay for the men, I suppose?"

"Of course. As well as something vague that they call better working conditions. But they want something else from us, too, Jessie. They want us to refuse to hire any men who aren't members of the Friends of the Working Man."

"Now, that's ridiculous!" Jessie exclaimed. "This is still a free country, and freedom means that any man can choose the organizations he wants to join, or stay out of all of them, if he prefers."

"Well, I'm just telling you what I've heard, Jessie. So far everything's been talk and rumor and gossip, along with a certain amount of trouble."

"Then they haven't come to you with any specific demands, have they?"

Stevens shook his head. "They've been trying to get our miners to join up first. All the trouble they're causing now is to show how much more they can create if we don't listen."

"I'm sure it occurred to you that the longer time we

let this outfit victimize us, the more time it's going to take to get things at the mine back to normal?" Jessie asked.

"I'm hoping this Friends of the Working Man bunch will give up if we just hold our ground for a while. Time's on our side, I'm sure of that."

Speaking of time had set off a reminder in Jessie's mind. With a start, she suddenly realized that she'd spent more time talking with Stevens than she'd intended to. She glanced at her watch again and saw that she had only ten minutes left before the time came for her to go to her room and light the lamp as she'd promised Ki.

"I think we've about exhausted the subject of the Friends of the Working Man for the moment, Bob," she said. "Let's wait until Ki and I have had a chance to talk about this and I've talked to a few people in Bismarck. We certainly need to know more about this mysterious group than we do now."

"Whatever you say, Jessie," he agreed. As he stood up and circled the table to move Jessie's chair, he went on, "You'll be at the mine again tomorrow, I suppose? Or do you want me to come into town in the morning?"

"I'll come to the mine," Jessie answered as she stood up. "It'll probably be in the afternoon. I want to ask some questions here in Bismarck first."

"Then I'll just thank you for such an exceedingly good dinner and go back to the mine myself," Stevens said.

Jessie nodded. They walked together to the hallway, and Jessie started up the stairway. She took out her key as she reached the second floor and turned down the dimly lighted corridor to her room.

Quickly she unlocked the door and went inside. She moved without hesitation to the bureau and felt on it until her fingers found the base of the lamp and the saucer of matches beside it. She took a match from the saucer and scraped it over the sole of her shoe. Then she lighted the lamp, adjusted its wick until it stopped smoking, and stood beside the bureau, waiting.

Chapter 6

Ki stopped at the corner where Meigs Street and Second Street crossed. A number of years had passed since he'd last been in Bismarck, and he wanted to get his bearings himself before going any further. What he was looking at now was strikingly different from his memories of the past, though unlike some of the ethnic neighborhoods he'd encountered in other Western cities, Bismarck's Oriental district had not yet begun to creep outside its boundaries.

Years ago, when Ki had first visited the city on one of his visits with Alex, the block between Meigs and Tyler had been occupied by only three small shops and a huddle of a half-dozen houses even smaller than the shops. Now Second Street was lined with shops and the block was packed with little dwellings that stood cheek-by-jowl. Dominating the entire block was a big Buddhist temple that filled the corner across the street from where Ki stood.

Although the evening was no longer young, a steady stream of people was entering and leaving the temple. It towered three stories high and stretched for almost a quarter of the block on both Second and Meigs Street.

The temple's cut-stone walls were crowned by a triple-tiered tiled *Yatsummuni* roof. The roof with its up-ward-curving eaves dwarfed every other building in the neighborhood.

Beyond the temple the small houses clustered. They were crammed tightly, with no rhyme nor reason to their spacing, and filled the entire block. A glance was all that Ki needed to tell him that most of the little dwellings had only one or two rooms.

Facing Second Street beyond the temple's wall a solid line of small business buildings stood. Most of them still showed lights inside, though Ki saw only a few customers entering them. Even those in which the windows were dark had lighted lanterns hanging above the doors. On the bulging globular lamp chimneys colorful stenciled ideographs identified the kind of goods or services which would be found inside.

There had been no teahouses on the street when Ki last visited Bismarck. Now they were as numerous as the gambling parlors and geisha houses that were his most promising targets. Though the walkways in front of the buildings were busy, they were not over-crowded. Ki was able to pick his way rather than push-ing through the men moving in both directions along the narrow board sidewalk. As he moved, he watched the ideographs on the lamp globes until he saw the one he had hoped he would find, the *bo* symbol that marked a martial arts *do*. He reached the small frame building and stepped inside.

An old Japanese man with a white wispy beard sat in one of the half-dozen chairs that stood just inside the door of the big cavernous room. He looked up at Ki and raised his thin eyebrows in a silent question as he let his hand fall to his waist and hooked his thumb into his black sash.

Ki had noted the old man's black belt at once. He replied in kind to the silent question that the oldster had asked. Lifting the front of his loose blouse, he showed the black belt which was knotted around the top of his own baggy trousers. Now the seated man spoke.

"What *do*?" he asked.

"Sakugawa," Ki replied. "And I am Ki."

With his hand on his belt, the old *do* master said, "I am Masabu." Then he smiled, showing a snaggle of yellowed teeth, and added, "You need no more learning than I do, Ki. The masters who taught us had equal skill. Perhaps you have just come to visit?"

"To visit and to ask questions, if you will allow me to," Ki replied. "From the wisdom of your venerable years, I can see already that you will give me good answers."

"No answer is good if it is not what the one who questions wishes to hear," Masabu told him. "But talk is dry, and I am tired from the lesson I just finished. We will have tea."

Masabu clapped his hands, and a moment later a Japanese girl wearing an obi came through a door set into the rear wall. Ki watched her as she approached, and when she came closer he saw that she was not as young as he'd taken her to be at a distance. Though she moved easily and her face showed no lines of age, he could tell now that days when she could be called a maiden were well behind her.

"What is it you wish, Grandfather?" she asked. She was looking at Ki as she spoke.

"Tea, Uemora. This young *karateka* has come to visit me."

"At once," she said, nodding. Hurrying back to the door by which she'd entered, she went through it and disappeared.

"You are from where?" Masabu asked Ki.

"From Texas. You know where that is, I'm sure."

Masabu nodded. "Far south from here and beyond the big river. You came to live?"

Ki shook his head. "I serve a lady whose father I served before her. When he died, he left her the business that he had here. You would know about them, the coal mine and shipyard and some ships and barges that carry river cargoes."

"Her name is Starbuck, then?" Masabu asked. When Ki nodded, he went on: "She has heard of the trouble at the mine and come to attend to it?"

"You know a great deal, Masabu." Ki frowned.

"I have been here a long time. I have friends and students who work in the shipyard and the mine, they tell me many things. But even before I came to America, I knew of Alex Starbuck. He was a good friend to our people. You would know that better than I do, Ki, if you served him long."

"I did," Ki said. "Many years. I don't have time to talk about Alex now, though. I must get answers to my questions quickly."

"Ask them, then. I will try to answer."

"What can you tell me about the men who are making trouble at the Starbuck mine?" Ki asked.

"Little. Perhaps too little. They are not from here, but from another place. They came here to get money from the miners, like the shoguns of our own country who take from the poor to make themselves rich."

"That much I know myself," Ki said, nodding. "I must find their names and where they stay and who gives them orders."

Masabu frowned. "I know nothing of those things now. The men who came here to steal stay by themselves. I have heard the name of their *do*, it is called Friends of the Working Man."

Ki did not bother to correct the old *karateka*'s mistake. He nodded and said, "I have also heard this. Do you know how many of them there are?"

Masabu shook his head. "I only know there are more than two or three, I do not know how many. I am sure it will be an easy thing to find out more. I have many friends who work at the mine and the shipyard, and others who serve in the houses of the rich people here."

"How soon can you find out, Masabu?"

"Little tonight, much tomorrow. But perhaps Uemora will know. She will be here with our tea in—"

Masabu broke off as his granddaughter came in. She was wheeling a serving cart that bore a steaming teapot and a platter of small cakes as well as small plates and the handleless cups of Japanese porcelain. Uemora stopped and bowed to the men in the Japanese style before placing cakes on the small plates and filling the cups.

Ki took the opportunity to study Uemora while she was busy. The long kimona she wore dropped in a straight line from her shoulders to her ankles, but now and then one of her deft movements pulled the fabric of the garment over the swell of her breasts. She finished filling the plates and offered them to Ki and Masabu.

"Is it permitted that I take tea with you, Grandfather?" Uemora asked when the men had been served.

"Of course," Masabu replied after he'd glanced inquiringly at Ki and received a nod in reply. "Our countryman has asked for information, my child. Do you know how many men there are here now of the *do* called Friends of the Working Man?"

"I have heard people speak of them," Uemora replied. "But I do not know of anyone who has counted them."

"Perhaps you could guess," Ki suggested. "Or perhaps you know someone who can tell you."

Uemora shook her head. "I do not know anyone. And Ahseta has told me that they talk to no one but themselves and a few of the men who work at the coal mine."

"Who is Ahseta?" Ki asked.

"My friend," she told him. "She works for Mr. Pendergast."

"Elzey Pendergast?" Ki frowned.

Uemora nodded. "She told me only a day or two ago of an argument between him and one of the Friends."

"What was the argument about?" Ki asked quickly.

"Ahseta did not tell me this. They were in Mr. Pendergast's office and the door was closed. But she said she could tell from their loud voices that they were both angry."

"What does Mr. Pendergast do here?" Ki asked.

"That I do not know," Uemora said with a frown. "Even Ahseta does not know. He works in his private room, and he sends many telegrams, but that is all I can say."

Masabu spoke for the first time since the exchange between Ki and Uemora had begun. "It would please me if you help our friend Ki," he told Uemora. "I wish to help him, for he is one of us. Ask questions of your friend, my child, and tell Ki anything you learn."

"Of course, Grandfather," Uemora agreed. "I will try to do what I can."

While Masabu and Uemora talked, Ki had suddenly realized how long his visit had lasted. He put his plate aside and stood up, turning to Masabu.

"I would like to stay and talk more with you and Uemora," he told the old man. "But Miss Starbuck will be expecting me at the hotel. I must go now, but tomorrow I will come back." He turned to Uemora and added, "If you can learn more about Elzey Pendergast, I would like to hear what you find out."

Jessie waited beside the bureau for a moment after she'd lighted the lamp, then she started toward the armchair across the room. She'd taken only one short step when her rifle caught her eye. Instead of going to the chair she stepped to the corner and took the gun out of its saddle sheath. Handling the rifle reminded her of her Colt, and she detoured past the dresser, opening the drawer where she'd put her gunbelt.

Carrying both the Colt and the Winchester, Jessie reached the chair at last. After settling into the deep upholstered seat she pumped a shell into the rifle's chamber and laid the weapon on the floor. She put the revolver on her lap.

Sitting comfortably, relaxing from the busy day she and Ki had spent, Jessie dozed for a moment, awoke with a sudden jerk, and realized that she must move around or she'd fall asleep in spite of her efforts to keep alert. She stood up and started away from the chair.

Before she could take a second step the crack of a small explosion broke the room's stillness and banished any thought of sleep. The explosion was followed by a brief but loud hiss and a stream of sparks spurting from the end of the fuse. The copper shell of the percussion cap that had been crimped on the end of the fuse arced in a shining flash across the room and buried itself with a muffled thud in the back of the armchair in which she'd been sitting.

By this time Jessie had blown out the lamp and was starting toward the window. The long drape that had concealed the fuse was smoking now and a jagged ring of red at the level of the windowsill was growing brighter quickly where the spurt of sparks gushing from the fuse-end had set it afire.

Jessie's finely honed reflexes were triggered by the threat. Three long steps took her to the curtain. She dropped the Winchester to the floor and batted at the drape with her palms until the last spark of the blaze was extinguished. Then she picked up the rifle and went back to the window. Pulling aside the drape, she stared into the night's blackness.

A quick glance told Jessie that because of the lamp-light's reflection on the windowpane she'd be unable to see anything through the glass. She stabbed the Winchester's muzzle through the glass. It shattered with a crack, and the tinkling of shards landing below while she was leaning forward, trying to peer along the alley.

Only the murk of night met Jessie's eyes. She squeezed them shut for a moment, then opened them to try again. Now she could see the windows of the building across the narrow alley from the hotel, but when she looked downward, the black murk still defeated her effort to penetrate its gloom. Then Ki's voice from the alley below broke the silence.

"Pull your head back into the room, Jessie!" he called. "I can see you against the building, and if I can so can the man who lighted the fuse!"

Jessie ignored Ki's words and raised her voice to ask, "Are you all right, Ki?"

"Of course I am!" he replied. "And I suppose that the man who lighted the fuse is, too! I tried to put a *shuriken* into him, but it was too dark to aim, and I missed him!"

"He got away, then?"

"I'm afraid so," Ki confessed. "There's no reason for you to come down here. I'll come up to your room."

"You're sure he was alone?"

"If there was anyone with him, they've gone, too."

"Then you might as well figure that we've lost him for right now," Jessie said. A tattoo of impatient rapping sounded from the doorway across the room. She called, "The hotel people must be roused by now, Ki. I think that's them knocking."

"Don't take a chance on it!" Ki called quickly. There was an urgency in his voice, a tone that Jessie seldom heard in it.

"Don't worry!" she said. "Just come on up."

Turning, Jessie started across the room. As she moved she drew her Colt from its holster. She stepped aside from the door, pressing against the wall, and raised her voice to ask, "Who is it?"

A man's voice answered, "Night desk clerk, ma'am. Trying to find out what this ruckus is all about."

"You have a pass-key, I suppose?" Jessie asked.

"I sure do. But your key's in the lock and I can't use it. I didn't figure to need a spider."

"I'll take my key out, then you can use yours to unlock the door from the outside," Jessie instructed him.

She removed her key. There was a metallic scraping as the man in the hall followed her instructions. Then he opened the door just wide enough to allow him to slip his head through and look at Jessie. She recognized the newcomer as the man who'd been on duty when she passed through the lobby and lowered the barrel of her Colt.

"You can come in," she told him, and as the clerk slid cautiously into the room, went on: "What this is all about is that someone in the alley behind the hotel tried to kill me."

"Now, ma'am—Miss Starbuck, if I recall—what would anybody be trying to kill you for?"

Before Jessie could reply, Ki spoke from the hall. "Take Miss Starbuck's word for it. Someone set a trap for her and she discovered it. There are four sticks of dynamite over there on the windowsill."

"Dynamite!" the clerk exclaimed. "There couldn't possibly be such a thing as dynamite in the—"

He broke off as Jessie stepped to the window and lifted the charred drape. The clerk's eyes bugged out when he saw the explosive sticks lying in an untidy crisscrossed heap on the floor beneath the window.

"My God, it is dynamite!" he breathed. "How on earth did it get there?"

"Obviously, someone found a way to get into my room when I was out," Jessie replied. "They left the dynamite hidden behind the drape and dropped the fuse down to the alley. Luckily, I found it and Ki took the fuse out. Then we set a trap to catch whoever put it there. That's why I didn't report finding it."

"I-I see," the clerk stammered. "At least, I suppose I do. But I can't understand how you can be so calm after such a narrow escape, Miss Starbuck."

"Perhaps it's because I live on a ranch in Texas, where we get used to unexpected things happening," Jessie replied. "Now, would you mind if I made a suggestion?"

"Of course not!" the clerk said quickly.

"This little disturbance hasn't seemed to alarm anyone in the hotel, or there'd be a crowd in the hall now," Jessie went on. "Why don't we just postpone any further discussion of this little incident until morning? I'll sit down with your manager then and among other things I'll tell him that I don't blame the hotel for any of this and I'll be very glad to pay for any damage that's been done. Then we can all go to bed and catch up with our sleep."

"Why, I—" the clerk stammered, collected himself, and went on: "I'm sure you've heard the hotelman's motto, Miss Starbuck. The guest is always right. If that's what you want to do, I don't see any reason why we shouldn't. I'll just go make my report; we'll let everything else wait until morning."

After the clerk had left, Jessie turned to Ki and said, "I didn't see any reason for staying up half the night, Ki. Do you?"

Ki shook his head. "No. Whoever it is trying to kill you is pretty sure to lie low for a while. I can't see any reason for wasting the rest of the night. I certainly don't intend to leave you here alone, though. Regardless of what we may think, whoever set the dynamite isn't going to give up and it might just occur to them to try again tonight. You go to bed. I'll sleep in that easy chair."

"You don't have to, you know," Jessie pointed out.

"Of course I know!" Ki replied. "But that isn't going to change my mind."

"Then I won't argue," she said. "By the way, did your visit to the Oriental district bring anything new to light?"

Ki shook his head. "No. My friend gave me an idea or two, and I've arranged for his daughter to do a bit of quiet investigation, so we may get some information soon about these Friends of the Working Man."

"I'm sure they're the ones that tried to kill me tonight," Jessie said. Her voice was level and calm, but Ki knew her well enough to sense the anger that lay below her words.

"Of course they are," he agreed. "And I've found out that they seem to have some sort of connection with our friend Elzey Pendergast."

"Now, that *is* interesting!" Jessie exclaimed. "If we can connect them with Pendergast, now—"

"Yes, I agree," Ki said. "What did you find out from Bob Stevens?"

"Less than I'd hoped to. But so far, we've just scratched the surface, and I—" A yawn interrupted her, and when she'd followed it to its conclusion, Ki said quickly, "Let's call it a day, Jessie. We may see things more clearly in the morning."

Stepping to the bureau, Ki blew out the lamp. There were faint sounds of rustling cloth in the dark room for a moment or two as Jessie made ready for bed and a soft exhalation of breath from Ki as he fought a yawn while settling down in the easy chair. Then the room grew quiet as they slept.

Chapter 7

"Before we go into the dining room for breakfast, it might pay us to look around in the alley, to see if our murderous-minded dynamiters left any clues as to who they are," Jessie said to Ki as they started down the stairs the following morning.

"I'm sure they've covered their tracks, or tried to," Ki replied. "But if you're not too hungry—"

"Putting breakfast off for a few minutes won't bother me. And I'm still angry about that dynamite trap they tried to blow me up with."

"Let's look, then," Ki said. "The only cover I could find was a little bit of space between two buildings. They were quite a distance from the fuse, and all I could see was the man's figure outlined against the light of the match he struck. I don't know whether or not he saw me, because he ran the minute the fuse started to sputter and hiss."

"You said you threw a *shuriken* at him. Do you think it hit him?"

Ki shook his head. "I couldn't tell, Jessie. You saw how dark that alley is at night. By the time I got into it, where there was room enough for me to throw it, he'd gotten a pretty good start down the alley."

"It's not like you to miss with a *shuriken*, Ki."

"That's another reason I want to look now, before people start milling around in the alley. If I hit him, he might've left a blood trail. There might even be a few footprints. The alley's not paved."

They'd gotten outside the hotel now and turned to walk the short distance around the building to the alley's entrance. The narrow rutted earth of the un-paved passageway was almost as hard under their feet as the brick-paved street. They made their way to the long expanse of the hotel's brick wall. The long spiral of gutta-percha that had formed the fuse's waterproof wrapping still dangled from the window of Jessie's room.

"I think I was very lucky," Jessie said, looking up at the broken windowpane of her room. "And so was the hotel."

"Whoever your enemy is, Jessie, he was certainly out to get rid of you," Ki commented. "And I wish I'd been able to find a better place to watch from."

He indicated the narrow slit they were passing. It seemed to Jessie that the gap was hardly enough to allow a cat to enter. She turned back to mention her impression to Ki, but he'd gone on ahead and was bending forward, searching the alley's rutted ground. When Jessie reached his side, he'd dropped to one knee to get a closer look at the faint impressions of boot soles that showed in the crusted earth.

"I think my *shuriken* might've scored a hit," he said, pointing to the ground.

Jessie scanned the dry cracked dirt for a moment before she saw what Ki was inspecting. It was a small dark dot, almost invisible in the crusted soil.

Jessie frowned. "Is that a bloodstain?"

"I'm sure it is," he said, nodding as he stood up. Then, bending forward, he moved a few short steps ahead. Stopping once more, Ki bent down again. This time he touched the earth with his forefinger and brought the finger to eye level for a closer look before going on: "It's blood, all right. And it hasn't dried yet. I think my *shuriken* did hit him."

Jessie had reached Ki's side by now. She looked at the small smear of red broken by the line Ki's finger had made as he pulled it through the dirt.

"It's a blood spot, all right, Ki. And my guess is that whoever you hit is going to leave a trail for quite a while."

Ki nodded, then went on: "This hard dirt doesn't absorb moisture at all well, but I'm sure now that I didn't miss with my *shuriken*. And as far as I can see, it's not lying on the ground ahead."

"We'd certainly be able to see it, if it's not too far from here," Jessie said. "It'd be shining. Why, it would stand out like a sore thumb on this bare dirt."

"Why don't you go back and have breakfast, Jessie," Ki suggested. "This might be a trail I can follow far enough to lead us to the dynamiter."

"If the *shuriken* was buried in him, he'd have to stop pretty soon," Jessie said with a frown. "He'd surely stop to take it out of wherever it lodged."

"Even if he did that, there's a good chance he'd still be bleeding for some time," Ki pointed out. "And with any luck, I might be able to track him all the way to wherever he was going."

"Then I'll go right on with you," Jessie told him. "Breakfast can wait."

Ki shook his head. "No. This is a job I can do faster

if I'm alone, Jessie. Besides, the hotel manager's going to be looking for you. It'll save time if you talk with him now. If I'm lucky and can follow this trail far enough to give us some idea of where that dynamiter was heading, we'll both be free to take the next step."

"Rooting the man out?"

Ki nodded. "Finding out now where he went is just the first step. And it'll be easier and faster if I take it alone."

Jessie saw the logic of Ki's thinking. She nodded and said, "All right, Ki. But if you do get a hint where we might find that fellow's hideout, I certainly want to be with you when we catch up with him."

Ki acknowledged Jessie's reply with a nod. He turned then and began looking for the next of the dried blood drops that marked the dynamiter's course. Jessie watched him for a moment, saw that he was still finding signs that would carry him farther along the trail. Then she turned and started back to the hotel.

Ki's prediction that the hotel manager would be looking for her was correct. Jessie had no sooner entered the lobby than he was at her side.

"Miss Starbuck!" he exclaimed. "I've been very concerned about you! Since the maid who went in to clean your room reported its condition, I've searched the hotel trying to find you or your companion!"

"I appreciate your concern, but as you can see, I'm quite all right, Mr.—"

"Moorehead, Miss Starbuck. Clarence Moorehead."

"Mr. Moorehead." Jessie nodded. "I couldn't see any reason for disturbing you or the other guests of the hotel last night. Neither Ki nor I were hurt, and there was no danger of the attempt to bomb my room being repeated."

"I must say, you're taking this attempt to kill you very calmly!" Moorehead exclaimed.

"Living on a large ranch in Texas brings some sort of small crisis to deal with almost every day," Jessie said with a smile. "And if it will relieve your anxiety, neither Ki nor I are any worse for the bombing attempt. Our interest was to catch the man who put the bomb in my room."

"Since you're back safely now, I take it that you haven't been successful?" Moorehead asked.

"It's too soon to say. Ki is still looking for him. I came back for breakfast, and to go on with the business that brought us here."

"Without even having notified the police?"

"There wasn't any reason for them to be involved at this time. In fact, I'd much rather they weren't brought into things right now."

"But I'm compelled to notify them!" Moorehead exclaimed. "Just a few months ago the hotel's owners took out a large insurance policy on the building and its contents. One thing the policy requires is that the authorities must be informed at once of any damage which might result in a claim."

"I'd suggest that you notify them, then." Jessie's voice remained calmly unruffled. "I'll be glad to give them a statement that the damage was the result of an effort to attack me, and that the hotel was in no way responsible for it."

Jessie's calm, almost offhand manner was having its effect on the hotel man. He looked at her for a moment, frowning, then said, "That's very accommodating of you, Miss Starbuck. I want you to know that I appreciate the way in which you're taking this. I'll have your belongings moved to another room as soon as possible. And in view of the trouble you've encountered while our guest, there'll be no charge for your accommodations or meals during your stay here—at least, I assume you do intend to stay in the hotel?"

"Of course. You're in no way to blame for that affair last night. Ki and I will be staying here until I finish taking care of the business that brought us to Bismarck."

"Well," Moorehead said, his voice showing his relief, "I must say that you're being very understanding about this. I won't detain you any longer, then. I'm sure there'll be some more discussion about this matter later, but I'll try to make sure that it won't interfere with your own business affairs."

Jessie smiled. "Thank you, Mr. Moorehead. Now, I'm going to have breakfast. Suddenly I feel very, very hungry."

While she enjoyed her delayed breakfast in the hotel's dining room, Jessie set her keenly honed mind to analyzing the events which had followed her arrival in Bismarck. That the effort to kill her had been made so quickly and efficiently after her visit to the mine indicated only one thing: a hardened and shrewd adversary must have been responsible.

Setting the bomb in place could only have been done by men who knew how to handle explosives, veterans of other similar jobs. Such men would certainly have assumed that she'd oppose their efforts, and would follow a militant course from the beginning. The bombing attempt was evidence of that, and carrying it out so soon after she'd arrived gave its own evidence, that the Friends of the Working Man was a group that was both very well-organized and totally merciless.

Jessie's mind was still busy trying to analyze her adversaries when she finished breakfast. She went out of the dining room door and turned into the corridor just as a man carrying an oversized load of boxes and cases as well as a heavy wooden tripod reached the door. He and Jessie collided in the hallway and most of his bulky load began sliding from beneath his arms and from his hands to clatter to the floor.

For a moment the man stared at his belongings, then as he turned toward her, Jessie exclaimed, "Oh, dear! I'm terribly sorry! I'm afraid I was so absorbed in what I was thinking that I didn't look to see if the corridor was clear! Here, let me help you."

"It's as much my fault as yours for trying to carry a lazy man's load," he replied. "And while I appreciate your help, I think it'd be better if you just let me pick up everything. If you don't handle photographic equipment very carefully, picking it up can do as much damage as dropping it."

Jessie had taken a good look at the man by now and was a bit surprised at his small size. He was not as tall as she was, the top of his head rose only an inch or so above her shoulder, and his form was on the same small scale. He wore a Dakota-crimped hat on the back of his head, a checked flannel shirt, leather-crotch riding trousers and heavy leather leggings over high buttoned shoes.

"Perhaps you'd like for me to call a bellboy for you," she suggested. "They'd probably know how to handle your cameras and things properly."

"I'll handle my gear myself," he replied politely but

firmly. "Though I turned into this corridor to look for a bellboy to show me the way to the room occupied by a Miss Starbuck."

"This is certainly a coincidence," Jessie said with a smile. "I'm Jessica Starbuck."

"You're the lady who had a bomb go off in her room last night?" the photographer asked, his eyebrows arching in surprise. "You certainly don't look any worse for it."

"It wasn't a bomb," Jessie explained. "Just some sparks shooting out of a fuse. My assistant and I had already taken the fuse out of a stick of dynamite when the cap exploded. All that happened was a little burst of sparks shooting out of the fuse. There really isn't much to take a picture of, Mr.—" Her voice rose inquiringly on the last word.

"Barry, Miss Starbuck. David Barry. I have a photographic salon here in Bismarck."

"I see," Jessie said. "I suppose the hotel employed you to make photographs of the damage?"

"As a matter of fact, it was the insurance company in Chicago that sent me a telegram asking me to photograph the room," Barry replied. "They'll use the images I send them to evaluate the claim for damages filed by the hotel."

"I must say, you're on the job very quickly."

"Time's very important in these matters," Barry said. "I must get my images before the damage can be repaired."

"Of course," Jessie said. She thought for a moment and went on: "If it will help you, I'll be glad to show you my room. And since it's on the second floor, I'll also carry some of your equipment."

"That would save me making two trips up the

stairs," Barry said. "And some of my equipment doesn't need to be handled too carefully. Suppose I carry the camera and the cases containing the plates and solutions and you carry the tripod."

"I'll be glad to," Jessie said. "In return, I'd like very much to watch while you take your—images, you call them?"

"A trade term, Miss Starbuck," he replied. "Most people call them photographs. There isn't a great deal to watch in the taking of images, though. The photographer's art comes into use during the coating and exposure of the glass plates, and later the development of the plates to get a negative image. It's then that the art comes in, transforming the negative image into a positive one."

"It sounds very involved and difficult, Mr. Barry," Jessie said as she lifted the clumsy wooden tripod and put it across her shoulder. "The stairway's a few steps back from here. Suppose I lead the way?"

Barry nodded and bent to pick up his big square cases. Jessie led him up the stairs and to the door of her room. She eased the tripod off her shoulder and unlocked the door, opened it to let Barry inside, then brought in the tripod.

"My camera mustn't move during the exposure, you understand," Barry explained. "And once the exposure's been made, it must be developed at once."

"You'll do that right here in the room?" Jessie asked. "I don't know anything about photographs or taking them or anything else, you understand. Aren't there a lot of chemicals and mixtures involved?"

"Only a few," Barry told her. "I've already coated my plates with collodion and silver nitrate. After I expose them, I'll run to my darkroom—it's not far from here, in the Dakota Block. As soon as I get there I'll wash them in pyrogallic acid and iron phosphate. That brings out the image. When it's satisfactory, I'll rinse the plate in potassium cyanide solution. That's to fix the image and keep it from fading. Then I'll wash it well and let it dry."

"And the image can be seen then?" Jessie asked.

"It can be seen, but the shades of light and dark will be reversed," Barry replied, shaking his head.

"And how on earth do you do that?"

"I'll coat one side of some fine thick paper with albumen. Then I put the glass plate in a frame and lay the coated paper on it and expose it to the sunshine for several minutes. That causes the image to be reproduced on the paper. After that, I put the paper in a bath of collodion and finally in a bath of sodium hyposulfite to make it permanent. After that all I have to do is rinse away the hyposulfite and let the paper dry to have my picture."

"It sounds terribly complicated to me," Jessie said with a sigh. "It must take a great deal of time and patience."

"Well, the whole process does take an hour or so," Barry told her. "But the result is worth the effort."

"I'm sure it is," Jessie said. For some reason she could not understand, the photographer's explanation had aroused her interest and stirred her curiosity. She went on: "I'd like to see some of your photographs, Mr. Barry. Would you be inconvenienced if I visit your studio some day while I'm in Bismarck?"

"You'd be most welcome any time," Barry replied. "And I'll be in town for the next month or so, working on the plates that I exposed on a trip I've just taken."

"Another insurance claim?"

Barry shook his head. "Not this time, Miss Starbuck. You see, I bought this studio from a photographer named Goff. He was very interested in photographing redskins. I suppose that I inherited his interest while I was working for him, because I've followed his example."

"That sounds very interesting," Jessie said. "I'll be even more interested in seeing your images. Now, I'll leave you to your work and get on with a few things I need to attend to."

Jessie was sitting across from Ki at a small table in the corner of the hotel dining room while he ate a delayed breakfast. Between bites, he told her of his efforts to follow the blood-trail left by the would-be dynamiter.

"I'm sure the man who tried to blow you up realized he was leaving a trail after he got to the sidewalk where he could see the bloodstains on the boards," he concluded. "And since I didn't run across my *shuriken*, I suppose he got it out of his leg or wherever it hit him."

"He probably put it in his pocket," Jessie suggested. "I don't suppose there are many people in Bismarck who've ever seen a *shuriken*."

"That's probably true," Ki said. "Except for a few in the Oriental quarter."

"There wasn't any indication of where he might've been going when you lost the trail?"

Ki shook his head. "It was where the business section begins to be mixed with private homes."

"And he could've been heading for either a store or perhaps a doctor's office," she went on thoughtfully. "Or for one of the houses."

"I had an idea that he might be going back to a

rooming house," Ki said. "There are several of them on that part of the street, mixed in with the stores."

"I don't suppose we have any sort of chance to find him, then," Jessie said with a frown.

"Don't be too sure," Ki cautioned her. "I thought that as long as I was there, I'd spend a few minutes looking around. It occurred to me that right there at the edge of the business district there might be a doctor's office in one of those old houses that've been converted to rooming houses and offices."

"And?" Jessie asked as Ki was chewing a bite of toast.

Ki swallowed his mouthful before going on, then said, "I didn't find a doctor's office, Jessie. But I did see something else that was very interesting indeed. There was a sign, a very small inconspicuous sign, in the front window of one of the houses I looked at. I thought it might be a doctor's name or something of that sort, but I was wrong."

"You're teasing me now, Ki!" Jessie exclaimed. "What did you see on the sign?"

"About the last thing you'd expect. It read 'Friends of the Working Man.'"

Chapter 8

"Ki, I can't believe that you've found the headquarters of that mysterious bunch so easily!" Jessie exclaimed. "Are you sure that's the place where all the trouble is centered?"

Ki shook his head. "It's too soon to be sure of anything like that, Jessie. It might be that one of the members of the gang simply has a sign out to show which side he's on. But no matter who lives there or what the sign means, we're going to have to look into it."

"We certainly are!" she exclaimed. "And without wasting any time!"

"I was sure that's what you'd say," Ki said.

Jessie frowned in thoughtful silence for a moment, then she went on: "I'd intended to go out to the mine again today and make a very thorough inspection of the tunnels. I want Bob Stevens to take me through every one of them, old and new alike. But that can wait until tomorrow. Now that you've discovered that house, we'll have to find out more about it."

"That might not be as easy to do as you make it sound," Ki warned her.

"Oh, I realize that," Jessie agreed. "In fact, it could be a better idea not to go to the mine and just watch that house today. Perhaps we can find out who lives there, and how many visitors go in and who they are."

"We can take turns watching, if that's what you want to do," Ki suggested.

Jessie had been following her original line of thought. She didn't respond at once to Ki's suggestion, but went on: "I'm anxious to find out more about these men who call themselves Friends of the Working Man, but my guess is that most of the activity in the place you found will be later on, at night."

"Jessie, the house isn't going to move," Ki reminded her. "It's not too late to follow your original plan and go to the mine today. We should be back a little before dark. I'll watch the house tonight, and you watch it tomorrow."

"Yes. That's the best thing to do," Jessie agreed. "Now that we've decided, I don't see any reason to put things off. If you've finished breakfast, let's get started."

As he had the day before, Bob Stevens saw Jessie and Ki as they drove up to the mine office. He came out while Ki was still reining the horse to a halt and gave Jessie his hand as she got out of the buggy.

For her inspection trip of the mine, Jessie had changed into the clothes she wore while at the Circle Star, often-washed blue jeans and a short jacket worn over a lightweight shirt. She'd bound her hair with a folded bandanna and slipped her feet into a pair of calf-high low-heeled boots. Ki had not bothered to change his regular rough-day garb, he still had on the loose trousers and baggy blouse that he favored at the ranch.

"I hope I didn't overstay my welcome last night, Miss Starbuck," Bob Stevens told her. "But I was enjoying getting better acquainted with you."

"I enjoyed our dinner myself," Jessie replied. "But it had a somewhat unpleasant aftermath."

"Really? What on earth could've happened in a friendly town like Bismarck?" he asked.

"Someone planted a bomb in my room at the hotel," she said. "And I don't call that a bit friendly."

"A bomb!" Stevens exclaimed. "Why, that's—"

"Hard to believe, I'm sure," Jessie broke in. "But it was very real. Luckily, I noticed it at once, and Ki defused it before the bomber lighted the fuse."

"You caught the man, then?" Stevens asked.

Jessie shook her head. "No. He got away in the darkness. But we'll catch up with him sooner or later."

"I certainly hope so!" Stevens said. "And if I can help you to run him down—"

"It could be one of the men who work here at the mine," Ki broke in to suggest. "I don't suppose there are any businesses here that use dynamite."

"None that I know of," Stevens replied. "We don't use any large amount, just an occasional few inches of a stick to fracture a rock formation that's blocking a stope. In fact, we don't use enough to order any sizable quantity. Two or three stores in Bismarck keep it in stock, so we just buy from them."

"I'll get their names before we leave," Jessie told him. Turning to Ki, she went on: "There can't be too many customers who buy dynamite."

"I can tell you a little bit about them," Stevens volunteered. "The riverboat captains buy quite a bit. In

94

hard winters ice dams form in some of the shallow places upstream, so most of the bigger riverboats carry a few sticks of dynamite to break them up with. Then farther upstream there are a few timber cutters working the pine stands. They float their log rafts down the river. Now and then a raft hangs up in a shallow place, and they'll set off half a stick or maybe a whole stick behind the raft. That makes a big wave that lifts the raft off the bottom and starts it downstream again."

Jessie nodded when Stevens finished his explanation. Then she asked, "Do you keep an inventory of the mine's dynamite?"

"Oh, of course," Stevens said, nodding. "Even for the little bit we use. And I'll see that it's checked today. But I can't imagine that any of the miners had a hand in what happened to you last night."

Although Jessie's opinion differed very sharply from that of the mine's manager, she decided not to waste time discussing it.

"Let me know what your inventory shows when it's been checked," she said. "And now let's get on with what Ki and I came here to do today. Bob, if you're not too busy, I'd like for you to take us down into the mine and show us the places you mentioned where there've been attempts to cause trouble."

"Of course," Stevens replied. "I'd better tell you now, though. Some of the old coal pillars that were knocked to shards have been replaced with timbers and all those we've found undercut have been shored up."

"That doesn't matter," Jessie said. "What I intend to do is to check the damaged places against the time cards the foremen keep. I have a hunch you might've overlooked doing that."

Stevens realized at once what Jessie intended to do. Each miner's time card would show the days and hours he'd worked and the tunnel in which he'd been working. His jaw dropped and he stared at her and Ki for a moment before regaining his composure.

"It should've been the first thing I thought about," he said. "But I'll admit that the idea hadn't occurred to me."

"Some of them would put false entries on their cards, I'm sure," Jessie went on. "Others wouldn't think of it. But if we can get a clue or two, it'd help us trace the troublemakers."

Ki had been silent during the conversation between Jessie and the mine manager. Now he said, "When Jessie and I go over the time cards, we'll be able to pick out the men who were working in the tunnels and shafts that've been sabotaged. Then we'll begin asking some questions."

"Yes, I can see what you intend to do," Stevens said. "It's such a simple thing that I'm ready to kick myself for overlooking it."

"Let's get started, then," Jessie said briskly. "I'm sure you have a map of the entire tunnel system. I noticed when we were out here yesterday that the mine still has only one downshaft, so we'll just start at the oldest tunnel and work our way down to the place where the men are digging now."

"I'll get the master map from my office," Stevens told her. "And perhaps we'd better take one of the straw bosses along with us. We might run into a place or two where we'd need help in doing some rough work."

"No!" Jessie told him. "And I don't want you to give any of the miners a bit of information about what we're doing. If they ask questions, just tell them that Ki and I are here on an inspection trip."

Stevens did not argue, but nodded in response. Then he said, "I'll go in the office and get the master map. We'll need miner's caps, too, not only to protect our heads, but to have enough light. It'll only take a minute."

"Then Ki and I will go along with you," Jessie told him. "I haven't had a really good look at your new building, and this is as good a time as any to see what it's like."

As they walked into the spacious office building the two clerks busy at their desks looked up curiously, but said nothing until Stevens gestured toward Jessie and Ki.

"This is Miss Jessica Starbuck, and her assistant, Ki," he said. "They're here from Texas to take a look at the mine." Turning to Jessie, he went on: "Jim Blake and Jeff Carson, Miss Starbuck. They're the ones who keep track of tonnage and payrolls and all the other figures you see in my reports."

While Jessie and Ki acknowledged the introductions, Stevens went to his own desk and took a roll of papers from one of its pigeonholes. He picked up a domed gutta-percha helmet from the chair beside the desk and stepped to the back of the office to get similar helmets for Jessie and Ki. Small lamps were attached to the fronts of the helmets.

"We'll be underground for a couple of hours," he told the others, then addressed the men at the desks, "Don't worry unless we're gone more than four. I'm not sure which of the stopes Miss Starbuck will want to inspect."

Jessie broke in to say, "If I recall the term correctly,

what you call the stopes are the tunnels leading off the shaft." Stevens nodded, and she went on: "We'll start at the first one and go down one by one until we've looked at all of them. I want to see everything, from top to bottom."

"It'll take about three hours, then," Stevens said. He turned to the men at the desks and said, "We'll use the old ramp going down, so the ore lift won't be tied up." Turning back to Jessie and Ki, he went on: "If you're ready, we'll head for the workings."

Jessie and Ki followed the mine manager to the head of the shaft. A heavy steel cable stretched from its huge sheave to the engine house and disappeared through a slot in the wall. The working end of the cable was visible for a short distance down the shaft, then it was lost in the murky gloom. On one side of the yawning shaft a zigzagged ramp let to the mine's depths.

"It doesn't look like much," Stevens remarked as he led Jessie and Ki to the head of the ramp. "But your father told me once that when he bought this mine, he was gambling on a hunch that the man who'd discovered and developed it was wrong about the extent and depth of the coal deposits."

"Yes, Father told me the mine's history, too," Jessie replied as they began walking down the first stretch of the ramp. "He used to say that developing a mine like this was a much more challenging gamble than sitting in a high-stakes poker game. Then he'd chuckle and go on to say that hitting a good lode in a mine brought better returns than any jackpot he could hope to win in a poker game."

"As it turned out, your father was right," Ki said. "I

remember that the first time I came here with him he debated for quite a few days before sinking this shaft deeper than its second level. Then he decided to push the shaft farther down and hit not one, but two more good coal seams."

By this time they'd reached the first adit, the black mouth of a square tunnel that opened off the shaft. Stevens took off his helmet and produced a packet of Beecher matches from his pocket.

"You needn't take off your helmets," he told Jessie and Ki as he scraped the match head over his bootsole. "I'll light your lamps."

Stepping up to Jessie he touched the match to the wick of her lamp, then did the same thing for Ki before lighting the lamp on his own helmet. He settled the heavy helmet in place.

"Now," he said, "we'll see what this old tunnel looks like. I'll admit I'm curious about it myself. I haven't been into the worked-out stopes for quite some time."

"How many of them are there?" Jessie asked.

"Only two," Stevens replied as he led the way into the shaft. "We're working three shafts at once now, since the town's grown so big and the number of steamboats that use coal has increased. Between the farmers clearing land and the amount of wood that's been used since riverboats began coming this far up the Missouri, the demand for coal is increasing every day."

"I should remember the number of men you need," Jessie went on. "But I don't, and I didn't stop to look it up before we left the hotel."

"Thirty, give or take one or two. We're on a broad

coal vein right now. I'm planning to fill these worked-out stopes as soon as I can."

Jessie frowned. "Won't that be expensive?"

"You'll be able to judge that for yourself," Stevens said. He gestured to the tunnel they'd entered. "Filling should make sense when you look at the pillars that hold up the soil above these old veins. There's enough coal in them—even more than enough—to pay for filling them."

As their eyes adjusted to the dimmer light and they reached the first supporting pillar, Jessie was surprised at its size. It was a long partition rather than a pillar, ten feet wide and a bit more than head-high. It stretched so far into the blackness that they could not see its end. On both sides of the pillar the tunnel had been widened to allow the miners to work the full width of the coal seam.

"We'll fill from the end of the tunnel to keep it from collapsing," Stevens explained. "And salvage the coal that's in the pillars as we bring the fill back from the point where the vein petered out."

"And the fill you've put in will keep the tunnel from caving in," Jessie said.

"It's the only way to handle the job," Stevens replied. "I would've started on it quite a while ago, but I wanted to be sure you understood what I planned, and I've been delayed in putting it all down in a letter to you. The job's a bit hard to explain when you're writing about it."

"Well, I certainly won't object to you carrying out your plan," Jessie said. "Go ahead, when the time's right."

While Jessie and Stevens had been standing talking,

Ki had gone ahead of them beyond the massive pillar. He rejoined them now and as he came up, he said, "Jessie, have you forgotten the appointment you made before we left the hotel? We won't have time to go any farther right now; we'll have to come back early tomorrow and finish it."

Accustomed as Jessie was to Ki's mannerisms, she hesitated only for a moment before answering him.

"I guess it just slipped my mind," she replied. "Are you sure we won't have time to go any farther?"

"Of course I am! We'll have to leave right now if you're going to be at the hotel to meet Mr. Davis."

"I really did miscalculate," she said. "My appointment just slipped out of my mind." Turning to Stevens, she went on, "Ki's right. As interested as I am in going through the mine, we'll have to wait until tomorrow to go any deeper. I'm afraid my forgetfulness has wasted a lot of your time, but it'll save time tomorrow, because I'll be able to start with a pretty good idea of what to look for after we get here."

"Don't worry a bit about it, Miss Starbuck," Stevens said as they started back toward the mine shaft. "I'm sure you have a busy schedule, and that attempt on your life couldn't've made things any easier for you."

In silence they trudged up the ramp to the surface, where Jessie and Ki passed their helmets over to Stevens and started for the buggy. After they'd gotten out of Stevens's hearing, Jessie glanced at Ki.

"You've found something, haven't you?" she asked. "Or you wouldn't've invented that excuse to get us away without rousing Stevens's curiosity."

"Yes. But I'm not sure exactly what I stumbled into.

101

I didn't take time to look thoroughly. I thought it might be better if we came back out here tonight, after the office is closed, and did a bit of investigating."

"What did you find?"

"I'll tell you on the way into town," Ki replied as they reached the buggy and got in. As he wheeled the buggy around onto the road to Bismarck, he went on: "I didn't want to say anything in front of Stevens. I'm sure he doesn't know about it, or he wouldn't've taken us down that tunnel—he'd've made some kind of excuse for not going into it."

"What exactly did you see, Ki?"

"Somebody—several somebodies, in fact—has been using that abandoned tunnel for a meeting place. And of course you know what my first thought was."

"That the somebodies have a connection with the bunch that calls itself Friends of the Working Man," Jessie nodded. "But what roused your suspicions?"

"First, I smelled tobacco smoke," Ki answered. "And I know that it won't hang in the air very long. I was surprised, because after what Stevens had told us, I thought it was very odd. If you remember, he'd mentioned that the tunnel was just an old one with all the coal taken out of it."

Jessie nodded, then asked, "So you looked farther?"

"Of course. There were eight or ten big flat boulders lying in a sort of half-circle, like they'd been used for seats. Then I got a glimpse of a big box of papers beyond the stones. And when I looked on the floor, there were fresh footprints."

"I don't suppose you could tell how fresh?"

Ki shook his head. "There were too many of them

to give me any idea without having enough time to study them. But there'd certainly been more than just one or two men wandering in there casually, Jessie. I'm only guessing, I'd say there were a dozen rocks that'd been used as seats. Maybe even more."

"And you didn't take time to look in the box of papers, of course."

"Certainly not. From what Stevens said, there wasn't any reason for the footprints or the tobacco odor or the box of papers, or the stones."

"You know what I'm thinking," Jessie said.

"Yes. Stevens obviously isn't aware yet that the old tunnel is being used for a meeting place. If he had been, he wouldn't have taken us into the tunnel at all."

"That's right," she agreed. "He said there were a couple of other abandoned tunnels between the surface and the ones where the miners are working now."

"He'd've taken us to one of the others," Ki nodded. Then he frowned and went on, "Unless he's playing some sort of double game at the moment."

"It's possible that he is, of course. But that's something we'll have to come back and look into. At night, when the office is closed there's only a half-shift of miners working."

"Exactly," Ki said. "I'll have to put off going back to Masabu's *do* to find out what he's learned."

"It's still early, Ki. We'd planned to stay at the mine a lot longer than we did. And we don't want to go back there before we're sure that all the men have left, and Stevens has gone to bed."

"Midnight or later," Ki agreed. "I suppose we can go ahead with the plans we've already made."

"Of course," Jessie told him. "Because by tomor-

103

row I'm sure that those Friends of the Working Man will have heard about our visit to the mine today. And if they're the ones who've been using that old tunnel as a place to talk to the miners, we just might find enough evidence in it to put a few of them in jail—if only for trespassing."

Chapter 9

"Changing our plans the way we did after your discovery is going to give us a little bit of spare time, Ki," Jessie commented as they began passing the small scatter of dwellings that stood on the outskirts of Bismarck.

Ki nodded and said, "We can use it. There are a few loose ends dangling that need to be tied up."

"But when we change plans we change our time schedule." Jessie frowned. "I thought we'd be getting back later, about the time when we could start watching that house with the Friends of the Working Man sign in the window. It's too early, now."

"We don't want to do that before dark," Ki agreed. He was reining the buggy into Main Street now. "But I do have one thing to keep me busy until then. I want to go back to Masabu's *do* and find out if his daughter's talked to the friend she thought might be able to give her some information."

"Her friend who works for the mysterious Mr. Pendergast?"

Ki nodded and said, "It's a little bit early in the day for me to go to Masabu's place, but I want to talk to

105

him for a few minutes. There's a chance that some of his pupils might be able to tell us more about those secretive Friends."

"It's worth a try, of course," Jessie agreed.

She glanced around as Ki tightened the reins to turn the buggy into Third Street. A sign hanging under the awning of the imposing three-story cut-stone building that filled the corner caught her eye. D. BARRY, PHOTOGRAPHY STUDIO, it read. On an impulse of the moment, Jessie turned back to Ki.

"Pull up," she said. "I know now how I'll spend part of my spare time. Mr. Barry's studio is in this building. I promised him that I'd stop in and take a look at some of his photographs—images, he calls them—and this is as good a time as I'm likely to have."

"That sounds interesting," Ki told her as he brought the buggy to a stop. "But I'd better go ahead with my own plans. If you don't mind walking back to the hotel."

"Of course I don't," Jessie assured him. She was getting out of the buggy. "It's not very far."

Ki slapped the reins over the horse's rump, and after the buggy had rolled away Jessie crossed the street. The sign that had caught her attention was hanging above a shallow passageway leading to a flight of stairs. She mounted the steps. At the second-floor landing a smaller sign, this one shaped like an arrow, read D. BARRY STUDIO.

Following the arrow's direction, Jessie moved down the hall to a door which stood ajar. She stepped through it and entered a long narrow room. Every wall was covered with photographs of all sizes and depicting the widest possible variety of subjects and people.

Indians dominated the assortment of pictures. The

redmen were of all ages, from papooses in their carrying cradles to old men with faces as wrinkled as relief maps. The variety of their faces was astonishing; so were their different hairstyles. Some of the Indians portrayed fitted the traditional appearance which Jessie had as a child attributed to redmen: sharp high-bridged noses like hawk's beaks, high cheekbones, craggy jawlines. Others verged on the negroid, with flat noses and flared nostrils; still others could have been mistaken for Orientals.

Their hairstyles differed as widely as their faces. Some wore twin braids drooping over each shoulder and trailing down to their waists. On others warlocks rose like brushes along the center of their shaven skulls, and a few wore their hair in a club-shaped appendage down their backs. Almost all of them sported at least one feather, some in a topknot, some in a headband. A few of those who'd been photographed standing had on full-feathered headdresses that trailed down their backs in twin or single lines down to the ground.

Some wore a garb of leather jackets and full-length leggings; others had on long leggings, and a few wore only breechclouts. None of the Indians depicted was without some sort of weapon. Bows and arrows were few; so were firearms. The most favored weapons were war clubs, tomahawks, and oversized knives. Several carried lances with flint points and feather-decorated shafts.

As she studied the faces portrayed, Jessie suddenly realized there was a single feature common to all the faces she saw in the portraits: not one of the Indians was smiling.

Her study of the photographs was interrupted by

David Barry. He came through a door near the rear corner of the long narrow room, carrying a half-dozen curled-edge pictures in his hands. He stopped when he saw Jessie and bobbed a little bow.

"Miss Starbuck!" he said. "I didn't expect you to be so quick in accepting my invitation."

"I had an unexpected bit of spare time," Jessie explained. "And just happened to notice your sign when I was passing by on the street, so I thought this might be a good time to stop."

"I'm glad you did," Barry told her. He nodded toward the array of photos on the wall beside them. "I see you've been looking at these of my Indians."

Jessie nodded. "They're very interesting. I've traveled in the West quite a bit, but I've never encountered such a wide variety."

"I think you'll find most of the important chiefs in the collection." Barry began moving from one of the Indian photographs to another, pointing as he talked. "These are three of the best-known chiefs of the tribes that defeated Custer: Rain-in-the-Face, Sitting Bull, and Gall. The one wearing the big feathered headdress is War Eagle, the next two are Old Wolf and Little John. The one at the far end is Curley, Custer's scout. That's Red Cloud holding the pipe and Chief Red Horse is next to him. I have a great many more, but no room to hang them in."

"They're certainly fascinating," Jessie said. "You must've been very busy, running down all those chiefs."

"I'll have to tell you that not all of them are my work, Miss Starbuck. Some were taken by Orlando Goff. When we were talking at the hotel, I believe I mentioned buying this studio from him."

"Yes, I remember," Jessie said, nodding.

Barry went on: "When Mr. Goff allowed me to keep these images on the wall, I promised myself that I'd carry on the job he'd started."

"Which you certainly appear to be doing," Jessie said.

Barry acknowledged her reply with a nod before going on: "The Indians defeated Custer, Miss Starbuck, but they also defeated themselves. Every fort the army has here in the West has been enlarged and reinforced. The Indians are being forced into a kind of life they can't survive. I'm making images of a people and their way of life that will both be gone before too many years have passed."

"Whoever took them, the images are all excellent."

"Thank you, Miss Starbuck," Barry said.

"One thing I've noticed is that even the smallest details show up in them," Jessie said.

"Of course. A good photographic image should portray even the tiniest wrinkle," he said. "It's a matter of recording the light and shadows—especially the shadows—on the negative. In fact, the Indians have given me a name, *Icastinyanka Cikla Hanzi*."

"And did they tell you what it means?"

"Either 'The Catcher of Small Shadows' or the 'Little Shadow Catcher.' My hunch is that the second version's correct, since I'm not as tall as I might be. But even if I'm not sure of the exact translation, I've learned to answer to the name they gave me when one of them addresses me by it."

Jessie smiled and nodded. She sensed Barry's pride in his images and that he'd been accepted by the Indians. Then she went on: "I think I could count the ribs in the feathers of some of the warbonnets the Indians are wearing in those pictures. And make out the embossed designs on the buttons of the soldiers' coats and the details of the insignia medallions on their hats."

"I pride myself on getting the sharpest focus possible," Barry told her. He held up one of the pictures in the stack he was carrying. "As you see from this image of your room at the hotel, the designs on the wallpaper and the embroidery on the draperies show very clearly."

As Jessie looked at the picture of the hotel room after the bomb fizzled out, an idea suddenly took full form. She lowered the photograph and said, "I don't know a thing about the technical details of your work, Mr. Barry, but tell me, would you be able to take your images in the tunnels of a coal mine?"

"I can make my images anywhere, Miss Starbuck. Of course, in a coal mine—" He paused thoughtfully, then went on: "I'd need light, of course. But there's a new magnesium powder now that gives off a short burst of exceptionally brilliant light when it's ignited. I'm sure I could make the kind of image you've asked about if I used magnesium powder."

"How would you go about it?" she said with a frown.

"I'd need to work out the fine points," Barry admitted. "I shouldn't have any difficulty, though. Why do you ask?"

"I own a coal mine a short distance from Bismarck," Jessie said. "There's a group of—well, I'd call them agitators—trying to create friction between me and the miners. Ki—you met him when you were at the hotel—Ki and I have discovered that they're meeting in an abandoned tunnel in my mine. I'm reasonably sure I'll charge them with trespassing and bring them to court. I'll need evidence against them if I do that."

"No matter where they're taken, photographic images tell their own story, Miss Starbuck," Barry said.

Jessie went on: "It occurred to me while we were talking that your images of them trespassing on my property, perhaps even while they're at work doing their mischief, and copies of documents that would prove they conspired to harm me would go a long way toward helping me win my court case."

"Copying documents isn't a problem," Barry told her. "That can be done anywhere there's light enough."

"I'd better caution you in advance," Jessie said. "There may be a bit of trouble connected with getting your images."

Barry smiled as he replied, "Trouble doesn't bother me. I happen to be a fair shot, and I doubt that I'd be in any more danger in your mine than I'd be in a village of any of the warlike Indian tribes. But if you expect trouble, I'll remember to wear my pistol belt."

Jessie was already thinking ahead. She nodded in response to Barry's answer before saying, "From what I've seen, you need a certain amount of time to place your camera and make adjustments and things of that sort. I can see that it'll take a bit of planning if this idea of mine is going to work."

"From what you've told me, it seems quite practical."

"I'm glad you think so," Jessie said. "But suppose we both do some thinking about it. I'll stop by again tomorrow, and we'll see what we can work out."

111

"I'm at your service, Miss Starbuck." Barry bowed. "I'll be here throughout the day, so stop in at your convenience."

Still thinking about her idea, and with fresh approaches occuring to her as she walked, Jessie returned to the hotel.

As Ki had anticipated, activity at that time of day in Bismarck's Oriental section was almost at a standstill. Three or four of the shopkeepers had brought chairs out of their stores and were sitting in front of the buildings, and fewer than a half-dozen people were walking along the street. He reined in at the narrow little building that was the entry to Masabu's *do* and went inside. Just as he'd been the evening before, the old martial arts master was sitting alone in the spacious room.

"Ki," Masabu greeted him. "You return earlier than I thought you would. It is good that you have come now, though. Uemora and Ahseta are in the house. Go through that door in the back. You and I can talk later, after they tell you the things they have learned."

Ki nodded and followed Masabu's directions. The door he passed through opened into a small hallway, and from the end of the narrow passage Ki could hear the murmur of voices. He went into the room. It was sparsely furnished in the Japanese style: two or three chairs set along one wall, a narrow backless bench on the opposite wall, and in the center several square padded mats pushed together.

Uemora and another young Japanese woman were sitting on their heels in Japanese fashion, chatting and sipping tea. Both wore gaily embroidered kimonas. A tray holding a teapot and several small handleless cups

112

was on the floor beside the mats. Both the young women looked up when Ki came in.

"Come and join us, Ki," Uemora said. "I have told you of Ahseta and her of you, so it is not like strangers meeting."

Ahseta twisted to her knees and bowed to Ki. He made a low bow to acknowledge Ahseta's greeting.

Uemora went on: "Both Ahseta and I have things to tell you. We will talk after you drink tea."

Ki crossed the room and hunkered down facing the two young women. Uemora had filled a cup while he was making his way to the mats, and she handed it to him now. Ki sipped his tea and the women watched him for a moment. Ki understood that they were waiting for him to drink, and sipped his tea in small quick swallows. When he'd drained the cup, he returned it to Uemora.

"I am refreshed now, thanks to your delicious Mo-Lai Fai," he said. "And I'm anxious to hear what you have learned."

"What I have found out is by accident," Uemora told him. "And perhaps it means nothing. But Grandfather has a student who comes to him early in the day. His name is Isida. This morning he was very late, and when he apologized he explained that a friend had come to him and asked if he was interested in earning a great deal of money. When Isida said yes, his friend took him to a small house on Sweet Street, by the riverfront, where a man he did not know offered them fifty dollars each to capture a man and a woman whose names he did not say. They were to take them to a place that he would tell them of later and tie them securely and leave them there."

Though Ki's expression did not change while Uemora was talking, his mind was working busily. When Uemora fell silent, he asked her, "This man, did he ever get around to telling your friends who the man and woman were? Did he mention their names, or where they could be found?"

Shaking her head, Uemora went on, "The man said only that he would tell them later."

"Did your friend agree to do what the man wished?"

"They have not had such a thing happen before," Uemora said. "Isida and his friend wanted to talk together first."

"Do you think they will take his offer?"

Uemora's voice was uncertain as she answered, "I think they will do whatever Grandfather tells them is best. He does not like for his *karateka* to break laws or to do anything that would give his *do* a bad name."

"I'll talk with your father about this later," Ki told her. "Right now, I'm anxious to find out what Ahseta has to say."

"I know very little, Ki," Ahseta said. "Mr. Pendergast is a man who does not talk much to servants. And in his private room, his office, there is a big safe that he keeps most of his papers in. It is always locked when he is away."

"Did you think of looking in his desk?" Ki asked.

"Yes," Ahseta said, nodding. "It is locked always when he is gone. But he writes many letters and gets many, as well. And there are a lot of men who come to talk with him. I do not know much about them, though, except that most of them look like they do hard work outdoors."

"Or perhaps in the coal mine?" Ki suggested.

"Oh, yes," Ahseta replied. "Some of them work

there. I know that from the coal dust that is still on their faces."

"Just keep watching, if you will," Ki told her. "I'm sure that Miss Starbuck will be glad to reward you for any information you bring her."

"And you, Ki?" Uemora asked. "Will she reward you?"

Ki frowned. It was not the first time he'd been asked about his connection with Jessie. Falling back on the explanation he always gave in reply to such a question, Ki said, "Her father was the one who took me from the life of a homeless *karateka*. I owe much to Jessie because of him. She is as my sister."

Uemora turned to Ahseta and said, "You see? I was right. Go lock the door to the *do*. Grandfather doesn't come in here often during the day, but we don't want to be interrupted."

As she spoke, Uemora was standing up, loosening the sash of her kimona as she rose. She shrugged her shoulders and the kimona slid to her feet, leaving her nude, an ivory statue.

"You have seen *shunga*, Ki," she said. "Now Ahseta and I will enjoy living *shunga* with you."

Ki had indeed seen the erotic scrolls Uemora mentioned, drawings depicting sexual scenes of trios and quartets, and in his youth as a traveling mercenary he'd encountered other women who enjoyed bringing them to life. He felt Ahseta's hands on his back, pushing his loose jacket over his head. Uemora stepped up closer to him and found the knot in the sash that supported his trousers. She pulled the knot free and pushed the loosely fitting trousers to the floor.

Ahseta's arms went around him and began removing the sash that he wore as a *cache-sex*. As he'd done

115

a moment earlier, Ki did not attempt to move or to stop her. While Ahseta's fingers were still busy unwinding the sash, Uemora pressed herself against Ki and started rotating her shoulders to rub the tips of her firm high breasts against his chest.

Ki could feel the dark rosy tips of Uemora's breasts grow firm as she continued to shift her shoulders. He did not try to halt the erection that he felt beginning. Uemora pressed more and more firmly against him, and after a moment or two she closed her eyes and her lips parted in a smile of anticipation.

Ahseta's efforts were at last rewarded when she stripped away the last binding layer of Ki's sash, but the one who benefitted from her efforts was Uemora, who could now lock her arms around Ki's neck. She lifted herself bodily while spreading her thighs to wrap her legs around his hips.

Ki had barely enough time to position himself to meet her when she tightened her leg-embrace and pulled his hips forward. Ki had already started his thrust, and the urgent pressure of Uemora's legs rushed it to completion. He lunged into a full penetration.

Uemora's small sharp cry of pleasure broke the silence as Ki went into her fully. She tightened her legs around Ki's back and started rotating her hips. Her head was lolling on Ki's shoulder and her arms were still around Ki's neck.

Ahseta stood up and moved to stand behind Uemora. She placed her hands under her friend's slowly rotating buttocks, and the support allowed Uemora to roll her hips more freely. Then Ahseta leaned forward over Uemora's shoulder and found Ki's lips. Ki parted them when he felt Ahseta's tongue seeking his. They

116

held their kiss only a few moments, for Uemora's wriggles were making it difficult for him to hold his balance.

"We must lie down," Ahseta said. "Can you kneel without breaking your bond with Uemora?"

"Of course," Ki assured her.

Summoning all his skill and muscular control, Ki managed to lower himself to his knees without breaking the bond between him and Uemora. With Ahseta's help he and Uemora moved to lie on their sides. Uemora abandoned their kiss and arched back from her waist, allowing Ahseta to bend and find Ki's lips.

As Ki and Ahseta prolonged their tongue-twining kiss, Uemora began shuddering and rocking her hips in response to Ki's more vigorous upthrusts. Ahseta's hands were caressing his muscular chest and back. Ki moved his hands from her to Uemora, stroking the pebbled rosettes of her breasts between moments of fingering Ahseta's moist depths.

Uemora's hips suddenly burst into wild uncontrollable gyrations, her body twisting and shuddering. Ahseta moved away to allow Ki to give his full attention to Uemora, who was tossing and wriggling to completion.

Ki did not release himself. He held his erection and was ready when Ahseta helped Uemora to slip aside. Then she crouched above Ki, her thighs straddling his hips and sank down to impale herself on his still-rigid shaft. Ahseta threw back her head. Her lips fluttered in a sigh as Ki ended his deep penetration.

"Now!" she urged. "Bring me to pleasure quickly so that Uemora and I can join in bringing you the same delight that you have given us!"

Chapter 10

"You were so late returning from your visit yesterday that I ate supper and went to bed without waiting for you," Jessie told Ki the next morning as she opened the door of her room for him in response to the light rhythmic tapping of his fingertips. "I hope your afternoon and evening were as productive as mine, Ki."

"It was late when I got back, and the transom over your door was dark, so I didn't disturb you," he replied. "And I've learned a few things we didn't know about Pendergast. But my feeling is that what I've found out so far has only scratched the surface."

"And surfaces often hide unpleasant things," she added, settling into a chair. "Right now almost anything we can learn about him is helpful, since we know so little about the man."

Ki leaned back in the chair he'd chosen and went on: "From what his housemaid told me yesterday, our Mr. Pendergast seems to be involved in a number of things. He's talking to the coal miners, he has quite a few visitors who don't fall into the classification of social guests, and he keeps all the drawers of his desk locked whenever he's not at home."

"You're saying that he's both busy and secretive," Jessie said with a frown. "And even before we came to Bismarck we knew that he was interested in buying all the businesses that Alex put together here—the mine, the shipyard, and the freight boats."

"And we've found out that he has the money to pay for them, or that he can get it from the bank," Ki added.

"We also know enough about him to suspect that he's involved with the Friends of the Working Man. What you learned yesterday confirms what we suspect, but we're still not sure that he's breaking any laws."

"And we don't yet know whether he's his own man or somebody's tool, but I think we agree that he's not interested in helping the miners," Ki went on. "He's just using them to make the mine difficult to operate. It's a move to force you to take any offer he might come up with."

"Even if we feel sure that's true, we'll still have to dig up the solid evidence to prove it," Jessie pointed out.

"Of course. Papers, letters, or eyewitnesses who'll testify for us, if you intend to take him to court. And it's up to us to find them."

"Perhaps that isn't as big a job as we're taking it to be, Ki. Yesterday afternoon while I was talking to Mr. Barry, I found out that he can take photographs in the mine."

"Inside? In the shaft and tunnels, where there's not any sunlight?" Ki frowned.

"He opens the camera lens and then sets off some magnesium powder in a metal tray," Jessie replied. "It gives a sudden flash of bright light."

"It seems we haven't been keeping up with advances in making photographic images," Ki said with a frown. "If Barry can get a picture of Pendergast meeting with those men in the mine, we might have the evidence we need to bring him to court."

"That's exactly what occurred to me," Jessie said. "But we need to find out a lot more than we know now. I've been doing some thinking since I talked with Mr. Barry, Ki. Suppose we get him to go with us to the mine—say tonight, when the office is closed and only that small bunch of miners are working."

"And have him get his camera in place to take the images of the men who're meeting in that abandoned tunnel?"

"More than that," Jessie said. "I'd like to have copies of anything useful that might be in those boxes of papers you discovered. There must be something important in those papers, or they wouldn't be hidden the way they are."

Ki nodded and said, "If we go early, we can put things back the way we found them. But we'll have to find out when the gang's going to meet."

"Can your Japanese friends help you find out, Ki?"

"Perhaps," Ki said. "I'll have to ask them. And getting ready will take some time, Jessie. Suppose we spend the day learning all the things we need to know, and try to set our trap for the next night the miners meet."

"That sounds logical," Jessie agreed. "If we—"

A knock on the door interrupted her, and she gestured to Ki to answer it. He went to the door and opened it. A bellboy holding a small silver tray stood in the hall. He extended the tray to Ki. A business card lay in the tray and Ki reached for it, but as he raised his arm the bellboy covered the tray with his free hand.

"That ain't for you, mister," the bellhop said. "It's for Miss Starbuck, and I got my tip from the gent that sent it up—he said to give the card to Miss Starbuck and nobody but her."

Jessie joined Ki and the bellhop at the door. When he saw her the boy lifted his hand and allowed her to pick up the card. He touched his forehead and turned to go. Jessie closed the door before looking at the card, then flipped it over in her hand and read the few words penned there. Then she handed it to Ki.

Ki looked at the engraved name first: E. PENDER-GAST, and turned the card over to read the few words penned on the back in small crabbed script: *"Please join me in lobby, Miss Starbuck. E. P."*

"It seems that Mohammed has come to the mountain," Jessie said dryly.

"Are you going to accept his invitation?" Ki asked.

"Of course. After letting him worry for a moment," she said with a smile. "I'm sure he wants to repeat that offer he made in his letter to buy the mine and the shipyard and riverboats."

"You haven't mentioned whether you're any more interested than you were when you got his letter."

"You know I'd've said something to you if I had been, Ki. Why should I be interested?"

"No reason that I can think of," Ki replied.

"But if our suspicions are correct and he's using that bunch calling itself Friends of the Working Man to disrupt the mine's operation, I'm very much interested in stopping his mischief," Jessie went on. "And if you can get to his house quickly, I'll keep him talking long enough for you to get there. Do you think you can

121

persuade the young lady you met yesterday to let you look around a bit in Pendergast's private office? Or am I expecting something that's beyond the realm of possibility?"

"I doubt that she'd refuse. Keep him here for at least an hour, if you can, Jessie. I'll move as fast as possible. As soon as I'm sure Pendergast's giving you his full attention, I'll go out of the hotel by the back door. That should keep him from seeing me and wondering where I'm going."

Jessie nodded agreement and left at once. Ki waited until he was sure that if he passed them in the lobby Jessie would see him first and detract Pendergast's attention, then followed her.

In the lobby Jessie had no trouble identifying Pendergast at once. He drew her attention as soon as she reached the bottom of the staircase, a man of bulky frame, wearing a business suit of expensive Scotch tweed and a gold watch-chain that was large enough to serve as a ship's cable spanning his bulging vest. His face was broad and a bit florid, the point of his short beard neatly trimmed. A hawksbeak nose started curving from bushy eyebrows and ended in thin high-cut nostrils. His lips were full and flabby.

"Miss Starbuck!" he exclaimed as he stepped up to meet Jessie when he saw her approaching. "I'm sure I'm not mistaken."

"No, you're quite right, I'm Jessica Starbuck," she said.

"I found out quite by accident that you were in Bismarck," Pendergast told her. "I've been wondering whether you got my letter, since you didn't reply to it."

"My decision to come here was made very quickly," Jessie replied. "If I'd written you before leaving the

Circle Star, my letter and I would have gotten here at the same time. Since the telegraph wires haven't reached Bismarck yet, there wasn't any way to notify you."

"That's of no importance now," Pendergast told her as he dismissed the subject with a wave. "But suppose we find a place where we can talk privately. A table in the dining room, perhaps? Or have you had your breakfast?"

"In my room," Jessie said. "But coffee or tea would be enjoyable, and the dining room's a bit more private than here in the lobby."

After they'd settled at a secluded corner table with filled cups in front of them and a steaming pot of coffee between them, Pendergast wasted no time in getting to the point of his visit.

"I hope you've considered my offer to buy your properties here in Bismarck, Miss Starbuck?" he asked as soon as the small interval required by courtesy had passed.

"My business policies are those my father followed," Jessie answered. "When I receive any sort of offer, I think it over at once, then set it aside briefly. Later on, perhaps after only a short time but often after a day or more, I consider it a second time. Then I make my decision."

"A very commendable policy," Pendergast said when Jessie paused for a moment.

Jessie picked up the thread of their conversation quickly. She went on: "I've even reconsidered your offer after we got here and I'd looked at the mine and talked to my local manager—Mr. Stevens, I'm sure you know him."

Pendergast nodded. "We've met. He appears to be quite competent."

Jessie nodded, then continued, "I've also thought about your offer after looking at the mine and just glancing at the shipyard from a distance."

"And I'm sure you've given some thought to the distance your interests here are from your ranch in Texas?"

"Distances are being closed very rapidly," Jessie said. "And while I live at the Circle Star by choice, I try to visit all the properties left me by my father at least once a year. Bismarck's been a bit off the beaten track until now because the river steamers can't always be depended on. During the winter the river this far north often ices over, and summer traffic is delayed by low water sometimes. However, the railroad's making distance much less important now."

"Then may I ask what you've decided, if you've reached a decision yet?"

"Oh, I've decided," Jessie said. Her tone was almost casual. "I don't propose to let any minor considerations such as travel problems keep me from holding on to all the properties my father devoted his life to developing, Mr. Pendergast."

Pendergast did not reply for a moment, but his expression did not change. Then he said, "We haven't discussed the price I'm prepared to pay, Miss Starbuck."

"I rarely make a decision to sell on the basis of the amount of money I'd receive for one of the Starbuck properties," Jessie answered. She pitched her voice to a tone of casual disinterest. "In fact, I might even consider buying a healthy timber stand or even another mine while I'm in the vicinity. Do you have anything among your holdings that might interest me?"

A sudden flush crept up Pendergast's face from his collar to his brow. He compressed his lips into an almost-invisible line and the bulges of his jawbones whitened as their muscles grew taut. He regained his composure quickly.

"I doubt that I have any properties here in Bismarck large enough to interest you, Miss Starbuck," he replied. "At least, nothing that I'd consider selling. In fact, as you must have gathered from my letter, I'm really only interested in buying."

"Yes, of course," Jessie answered.

As she spoke she glanced at the little Tiffany watch that hung by its brooch-pin below the collar-line of her jacket. The swift flick of her eyes told her that Ki had not been gone on his mission long enough to bring his investigation to an end and went on quickly to buy him some extra time.

"But suppose I offered to buy your Bismarck properties and put you in charge of operating them as well as the mine and shipyard and riverboat fleet? And any other of my ventures that might follow, I should add."

Pendergast's jaw had begun to drop midway of Jessie's question. He caught himself up quickly. By the time she'd finished talking, he'd regained his composure.

"I think I'll not answer you at present, Miss Starbuck. If you have an offer of that sort which you're considering making me, I'd like to see it detailed rather fully in writing before I give you a reply."

"Of course you would," Jessie said. "And I didn't expect an immediate answer. It's a question both of us should consider quite fully. But since we're together and discussing the idea, there certainly won't be a better time for us to have a brief visit. Shall we just sit and chat a few minutes longer?"

Again Jessie could see that she'd taken Pendergast by surprise. He did not reply at once, then he smiled.

"Of course," he said. "This is an excellent chance for us to become a bit better acquainted."

"And, if we should decide that some sort of association in the future might be mutually profitable, it'll be a bit easier to resume our talk later," Jessie said with a nod.

Ki wasted no time in getting to Pendergast's residence. He did not go to the front door, but stood in the street for a few moments, looking for signs of movement inside the house. Within a very short time he saw a flicker of movement at one of the windows on the upper floor, and on the chance that the half-visible shape he'd glimpsed was that of Ahseta, he tossed a pebble to the windowpane. When the window was raised, he breathed a sigh of silent relief when he saw his guess was correct.

"Ki!" she called. "What are you doing here at this time of the day?"

"I must ask you a favor, Ahseta," he replied. "But we can't talk so loudly. Can you come to a door or a window on the first floor and talk with me for a moment?"

"Yes," she said. "Go to the side where the drive is to the carriage house. I will be there very soon."

Ki circled the front of the house and stepped into the porte cochere. After he'd waited for a moment the side door opened and Ahseta came out. Before he could greet her, she repeated her question.

"What favor have you come to ask of me, Ki?"

"Tell me first, the room you described yesterday when you were telling me about Pendergast's habits, does it have a transom?"

"Of course. All the doors do, except those to closets. How else could the house be kept cool in summer?"

"Will you show me the door to his private room, then?" The one where he has his desk and papers?"

"You haven't come to steal, have you, Ki?"

"Of course not! But Jessie needs to know more about this Pendergast. He's no friend of hers, or of mine, either."

"But I've told you that Mr. Pendergast locks his desk and the cabinet he keeps his papers in," she protested.

"I haven't forgotten, Ahseta. But I learned many things when I was a wandering *karateka* living by my wits. Perhaps I can open them. Will you take me to the room they're in?"

"And how will you get into a locked room?"

"Through the transom. That's why I asked about the doors."

"There's nobody but me and the cook in the house now," Ahseta said thoughtfully. She was speaking to herself as much as to Ki. Then the perplexed frown that had been on her face vanished. She smiled and went on: "Come, Ki. After the pleasure you gave me yesterday, I can refuse you nothing."

Ki followed Ahseta through the silent house to a door in the hallway that led off the ornately furnished living room. He glanced up at the transom and saw that it was open widely enough for him to slip through the vee-shaped gap. He turned to Ahseta.

"Will you watch here by the door?" he asked. "It

would help me, but I don't want to put you in danger or harm or risk you losing your job here."

She nodded. "I will watch. And if Mr. Pendergast comes in, I will whistle like a small dove."

"Good," Ki said.

He stood with his back to the wall across from the door, measuring distances with his eyes, then with a push of one foot against the wall behind him to give him momentum, he leaped for the upper doorsill. As he arched through the air he bent forward and reached to grasp the sill of the transom.

Ki swung on it for a moment before levering himself to a crouch, his arced back brushing the hall ceiling. Then with the ease of bending and twisting that was part of the life he'd devoted to mastering the movement of each muscle in his compact form, he pushed his head and shoulders through the vee. The strip of picture molding that circled the room between its ceiling and the transom was within reach now. Ki twisted to hang by his fingertips on the strip of molding, then dropped to his feet on the carpeted floor.

For a moment Ki stood motionless, letting his eyes grow accustomed to the changed light in the big room. A massive flat-topped desk dominated the high-ceilinged chamber. Behind the desk there was a high-backed leather-upholstered chair; at one end of the desk a smaller chair. Two or three small chairs had been pushed against the walls.

A pair of filing cabinets stood against one wall, their slatted front openings closed. Ki wasted no time on these, but went directly to the large desk in the center of the room. Its top was bare except for a large rectangle of blotting paper, a calendar, and an ornate silver holder for an inkwell and pens. Ki was about to turn away when the corner of a slip of paper sticking out of the calendar's pages caught his eye.

He lifted the pages and glanced at the strip of paper. His eyes narrowed when he saw that it had been torn from the top of a sheet of letterhead which bore the familiar imprint of the coal mine. The few scribbles on it had obviously been made hastily, but after puzzling over the scrawled lines for a moment he translated them: *Mtg—tun—Fri mdnt.*

Frowning thoughtfully, Ki returned the slip to the position in which he'd found it and devoted his attention to the desk's drawers. He tried to open each drawer in turn, but all were locked.

During the long years when he and Jessie were battling the cartel, Ki's skill had been called on before to open similar desks. Dropping to his back on the floor, he pushed himself under the wide center drawer and began feeling along its back end. He found what he'd been seeking and pulled at the thin rod which held the side drawers closed. It gave easily. Ki scooted out of the cramped position he'd been in and got to his feet before opening the first of the side drawers.

A green-enameled metal lockbox was all the drawer contained, and when Ki tried its lid, it opened easily. A long narrow brown envelope lay atop the small mounds of gold and silver coins and two packets of currency that were in the bottom of the box. Ki opened the unsealed envelope and took out a sheaf of narrow slips of paper that had been pinned together at one corner.

When Ki saw what he was holding he blinked unbelievingly. The top slip was a receipt for one thousand dollars. It was signed by Bob Stevens. Thumbing through the slips, Ki found that they were identical except for the dates, which were spaced a month apart. He studied the sheaf for a moment, then pulled out the pin that held them together and drew one out of the center of the stack.

Ki folded the receipt and slid it into the leather arm sheath containing his *shuriken*. Then he replaced the pin very carefully and returned the remaining receipts to the lockbox before putting it in the drawer and pushing it closed.

Now Ki turned his attention to the middle drawer. A pad of printed forms lay on top of a hodgepodge-heaped scattering of similar forms. Bending close, Ki read the words that appeared in bold-faced type at the top: MEMBER: FRIENDS OF THE WORKING MAN. The legend in small type that filled the remainder of the page was almost unreadable, and he wasted no time on it, but tore off the top sheet and added it to the canceled check in the *shuriken* case. Then he replaced the pad and closed the drawer.

Just as Ki reached down to open the third drawer, a light tatto of fingertip tappings sounded at the door. It was followed by Ahseta's worried voice.

"Ki! Come quickly! Mr. Pendergast has come back!"

Chapter 11

Ki covered the distance from the desk to the door in three agile leaps. A fourth leap, upward this time, lifted him to the transom's frame. He levered his legs through the top and landed with a springy jump on the carpeted floor of the hall.

"Hurry!" Ahseta urged, grasping his arm. "I have opened a window in the dining room that you can go out. It's on the side of the house which Mr. Pendergast cannot see. He's putting his horse in the stable now—he will come in by the same door you did. But you must leave quickly."

As she spoke, Ahseta was tugging at Ki's sleeve. He followed her along the hall to the dining room. She pointed to one of the windows that was open and ready, its curtains pulled aside.

Ki crossed the room at a run and dived headfirst through the window. As he fell he twisted his body to land on his feet. One quick step took him to the shelter of the shrubbery that filled the bed along the side of the house below the window.

As he hunkered down he heard the thud of the window being closed by Ahseta. By that time Ki was hidden, a shapeless unidentifiable bulk in the thick growth. He stayed concealed long enough to be sure that Pendergast had gone inside the house. Then he angled across the yard to the street and walked briskly back to the hotel where he went directly to Jessie's room and tapped.

"I'm sorry that I couldn't manage to keep Pendergast here any longer than I did, Ki," she said as she opened the door.

"There was no harm done, but I'm sorry he got back to his house so soon. I'd made a few very interesting discoveries, and I'm sure there are a lot of other things in his study we'd be interested in seeing that I didn't have time to uncover."

"I couldn't do a great deal to hold him," Jessie went on. "He suddenly got into a tremendous hurry, even though I tried to keep him interested. I even hinted that I might ask him to join me in developing some other properties here in Dakota Territory."

"I hope you weren't considering that offer seriously."

"Of course I wasn't! All I'd be doing would be giving him a license to steal from me, Ki! I'm not as gullible as I hope he took me to be, and I'm not as hungry for money as he is. My offer was bait, nothing more. I wanted a yardstick that I could use in measuring our Mr. Pendergast's motives."

"I take it that he didn't measure up?"

"Not even by a quarter of an inch. I'm more certain than ever now that the man's a swindling crook."

"More than that, Jessie. He's behind the Friends of the Working Man."

"Are you sure of that?"

"Quite sure," Ki said firmly. "I didn't have time to

find any of the details of whatever scheme Pendergast's trying to bring off, but he's certainly deep in plotting. I was going through his desk when he got back."

"How did you manage to get away without him seeing you?"

"Ahseta was watching for Pendergast," Ki replied. "She warned me in plenty of time that he'd arrived."

"You said you didn't have time to find out any details of whatever scheme he's got in mind," Jessie said. "Exactly what did you uncover?"

"Two or three quite surprising things, Jessie. I'm sure there's more to find. I was careful not to leave any traces of my visit, so if it's necessary I can go back the first opportunity I have."

As Ki spoke he was taking out the two bits of evidence he'd uncovered. He passed the check to Jessie first. After she'd unfolded it and glanced at it, she raised her head to look at Ki. Her eyes were snapping with anger and so was her voice when she spoke.

"Bob Stevens has been pulling the wool over our eyes, Ki! After our first visit to the mine, I'd have sworn he wasn't that kind of man, so it's a bit of a shock to learn that he's been selling me out!" she exclaimed. "And cheaply, at that!"

"Not as cheaply as you might think, Jessie," Ki told her. "That check came from a lockbox in Pendergast's desk. There was quite a stack of them, perhaps a dozen more. I didn't take time to count them, but I pulled this one from the center of the bunch. They were all pinned together. I'm sure Pendergast won't notice one is missing."

"Did you count how many checks Bob's gotten from him?"

Ki shook his head. "No. I was trying to work fast and wanted to get to the next drawer. It was almost as rewarding as the other one." As he handed Jessie the Friends of the Working Man membership certificate, he went on: "There were a lot of these in the drawer. I took this one from the top of a pad of blank ones. The others were all filled out."

Jessie unfolded the piece of paper and glanced at it. Aside from the "Friends of the Working Man" heading that was printed in bold letters at the top, there were lines for the member to fill in a name and address, and below them a paragraph headed RULES AND AIMS. Jessie began to read these, but after she'd scanned the first few lines, she turned to Ki.

"This is very interesting," she told him. "And a little bit scary, too."

"In what way, Jessie?"

"It seems this outfit only has three rules," she replied. "And just listen to them." She began reading: "One, all orders given by the leaders of Friends of the Working Man must be obeyed without questions or arguments. Two, members must report to the leaders when told to do so, whether day or night. Three, business matters at all meetings and orders are to be kept secret from outsiders."

Jessie looked up from the slip of paper. Ki said, "That sounds to me like the rules of some of the outlawed secret societies of Japan, Jessie. Their members almost tore my homeland apart."

"Now listen to what's on the other side of the paper, Ki," Jessie went on. "It's the oath the members of this outfit take." Reading from the slip, she went on, "As a member of the Friends of the Working Man, I swear before God and witnesses that I will follow my leaders without any question and will do any job they order me to do, even to ridding the world by force if necessary of the rich unfeeling bosses who oppress working men. I also swear to keep secret forever the names of my comrades in this war for justice and to tell nobody that I am a member who has sworn to carry out this oath."

"Why, that's a declaration of war!" Ki exclaimed.

"Yes, that's my impression, too," Jessie agreed. "What Elzey Pendergast is doing is making slaves of the men who join this outfit. He's forming it into a weapon that will allow him to ruin any business he wants and buy it dirt cheap."

"I wish I'd had time when I was in Pendergast's office to copy the names that were on those other membership forms," Ki said. "But he got there too soon."

"They had the names of the members on them?"

Ki nodded as he replied, "I thought about looking at some of them, but they were just in a loose heap, too many for me even to think about going through them. As things turned out, Pendergast came home just as I was starting to open another of his desk drawers."

"Those two you opened were quite enough, Ki. We've learned that Pendergast apparently has a number of tricks up his sleeve. If I don't agree to sell him the Starbuck property here in Bismarck, he's obviously out to force me to."

"And apparently he plans to use the coal miners as a sort of private army, just as soon as he has enough of them signed up as members of this Friends of the Working Man," Ki added, frowning.

"Do you think they'll fall for a scheme as transparent as that? Telling the miners he can get them more money if they'll join his organization, when all he wants them for is a smokescreen and free manpower to put the mine in such a state of turmoil that I'll sell it to him at his price?"

"His scheme will only work as long as he manages to fool them by hiding what he's really after," Ki replied.

A thoughtful frown had been forming on Jessie's face as they talked. Her voice reflected her thoughtfulness as she went on: "We've got to find out more about this outfit that Pendergast's putting together, Ki. It's quite obvious that the mine's at the center of his schemes, and now that we've found out a little bit of what's going on, we need to look for those who must be involved in it besides Pendergast and Bob Stevens."

"I made another discovery, Jessie," Ki told her. "I just haven't gotten around to passing it on to you until now. I'm sure I figured out what it means, and it might give us a chance to do exactly what you have in mind."

As he spoke, Ki moved to the little writing desk that stood against one wall of the room. Taking a sheet of hotel stationery from its drawer, he dipped the pen in the ink bottle that was on top of the desk. Bending down, he wrote the cryptic lines that he'd memorized from the slip of paper he'd found in Pendergast's calendar: *Mtg—tun—Fri mdnt*.

"See if you translate this the same way I did," he said as he handed the paper to Jessie.

Jessie studied Ki's neat lettering and a frown started to form as her lips moved while she was converting the abbreviated entries. The frown became an expression of anger which cleared away as she looked up and told Ki, "I make it out as 'Meeting—tunnel—Friday midnight.' But—tell me more about it, Ki. I'm very curious."

"I memorized what's written there from a slip of paper that was stuck into Pendergast's desk calendar. I didn't bring the paper, he'd have missed it at once."

Jessie nodded. She asked, "You got the same meaning from it that I did, I'm sure."

"Of course. My translation was just the same as yours, but I still haven't told you the most important part. The slip of paper those scribbles were written on was the top of a torn sheet of letterhead the mine uses."

"Bob Stevens!" Jessie exclaimed.

"Exactly," Ki agreed. "He must've written the note very hurriedly, or was trying to disguise his handwriting, because I didn't recognize his handwriting when I first looked at it. After I'd deciphered it, I certainly wasn't going to take the paper. If I'd done that, Pendergast would know immediately that someone had been in his private office."

When Jessie nodded absently, her expression thoughtful, Ki fell silent. He knew that Jessie was thinking through the problem as well as the challenge provided by the note. At last her face cleared and she looked up at him.

"Today's Friday, Ki," she said. "So unless this note was written last week or even earlier, this is our chance to find out more about Pendergast's mysterious Friends of the Working Man. All we have to do is hide close to the head of the mine shaft and watch to see who these men are."

"That means doing a lot of watching and trailing, Jessie," Ki pointed out. "There are only two of us, and we don't know yet which of the men at the mine are being paid by Pendergast—in addition to Stevens, that is."

"I didn't have watching and trailing in mind," Jessie told him. "There's a better way to find out. I'm sure they'll be meeting in that abandoned tunnel you went into at the mine. It's obviously been turned into a sort of headquarters for these Friends. It'd be easy for Bob Stevens to arrange that. In fact, it might have been his idea from the beginning."

"I can see that you've been working on the plan you were just starting to tell me about when we were interrupted this morning," Ki told her. "But go ahead."

"What we need to do right away is to find out which of the miners are mixed up with Pendergast's outfit."

"How much help will that be, Jessie? Do you plan to fire the ones who belong to this Friends of the Working Man that Pendergast and now apparently Bob Stevens have put together?"

Jessie shook her head. "That wouldn't be a good idea, Ki. What I have in mind is to convince them that they don't need to band into some kind of secret society to get fair treatment from any business that carries the Starbuck name."

"And you think that's possible?"

"It will be, if I get rid of Bob Stevens and refuse to make any sort of deal with an outfit controlled by Pendergast."

"But that'd mean you'll have to be here—or have somebody who'll be loyal to you running the mine."

"I'll be able to find the man I need at one of our copper mines or gold mines, Ki. And I'll promise these men here that they'll be listened to if they think they're getting treated unfairly. I'll give each of them a stamped envelope addressed to me at the Circle Star, so they can write me any time they feel I should know about something they think is unfair."

"Well, that certainly sounds practical," Ki said. "But how do you expect to carry out your plan, Jessie? You've got this outfit of Pendergast's to deal with first."

"Yes, of course," Jessie agreed without hesitation. "And I need to find out which of the miners are ringers brought in by Bob Stevens and Pendergast. I doubt that there'd be more than a half-dozen. It only takes a few to start something like this Friends of the Working Man outfit."

"How do you plan to go about finding the men we're after?"

"I'm going to ask Mr. Barry to help us do that."

"Your Little Shadow Catcher? How can he help?"

"By making an image, or maybe more than just one, of this meeting that Bob and Pendergast are having tonight. I'm sure all the men they've brought in will be there."

"That would certainly show you who's on Pendergast's side," Ki agreed. "But do you really think Barry can make an image in the dark, in that old tunnel?"

"After seeing his pictures and talking to him—and you didn't have a chance to do either—I'm sure he can, Ki." As she spoke, Jessie was glancing at the watch pinned to the breast of her jacket. "He's probably at his studio by now. Let's go have a talk with him."

"Why, I don't see any real problems in taking images in such a place as you're talking about, Miss Starbuck," David Barry said after listening to Jessie's explanation of the job she had in mind. "In fact, I'll be

139

very interested in getting more experience with exposing for images in the sort of place you've described to me."

Ki frowned. "And you're sure you can take images in a place like that mine tunnel, where there's no sunlight at all?"

"Quite sure, Ki. I've had a little experience using this new magnesium powder in dimly lighted rooms, but never in a place where it will provide all the illumination."

"Could you take pictures of documents as well as people in the dark?" Ki went on.

"Of course," Barry assured him. "All I'd need to do would be to adjust the amount of light that passed through my lens."

"I see what you're getting at, Ki," Jessie said. "Those boxes of papers you found in that tunnel where this meeting is going to be held."

Ki nodded. "If we go out to the mine early enough, there'd be time for him to copy them with his camera."

"And I'd welcome the chance to be sure my exposures are right later on," Barry put in.

Turning to Barry, Jessie said, "You have everything on hand that you'll need to work with, I hope."

"I have plenty of magnesium powder and unexposed film on hand," Barry nodded. "And if you want some images of documents I'd be able to judge my exposures better later. Of course, I'll need a bit of help in changing plates. I hope you and Ki won't mind lending me a hand—"

"But neither of us knows anything about making images!" Jessie broke in.

"You won't need to know anything about the actual image-making, Miss Starbuck," Barry explained. "I'll attend to the technical part of the job. What I need is to have someone standing ready to hand me a holder loaded with a sheet of unexposed film and take the one I've just used and put it aside in a safe place."

"I think we can be trusted to do that, Jessie," Ki put in. "Don't you?"

"I'm sure we can," she agreed. "Especially if you and I go out to the mine early, within the next hour or two. We'll need to get our bearings in that abandoned tunnel so that we won't waste any time later on."

"I'd like to go along with you," Barry suggested. "If I know what to expect tonight, I can plan in advance where to place my camera and what the focal distances are that I'll need to adjust for. That will tell me how much exposure I'll need so I can judge the proper amount of magnesium to use in my charges, things of that sort."

"That won't be a problem," Jessie assured him. "The tunnel will be deserted until just before midnight. We have a lot of time ahead—all we need to plan and get ready."

"Suppose Stevens sees us, Jessie?" Ki said, frowning. "He'll be sure to, unless we wait until the mine office closes."

"That's easy to avoid, Ki," Jessie replied. "I'll simply send a message to him asking him to come to the hotel and wait for me. I don't think he'll disobey an order like that—he must realize by now that he's skating on very thin ice."

Ki nodded. "And we can circle around to the mine by the riverfront road. Yes, that'll solve the problem. And we don't want to go to the mine office to get those helmets with lights on them, so while you're writing the note, I'll go to the nearest hardware store and buy a lantern."

Barry's head had been turning from Jessie to Ki as he listened to them planning their moves. Now he said, "Somehow, I get the idea that this isn't the first time you two have had to make quick plans in an emergency."

"Ki and I have worked together a long time, Mr. Barry," Jessie said with a smile.

Barry nodded and went on: "I've had a bit of experience in meeting emergencies myself. Occasionally when I'm out in Indian country I'll run into some of the wild ones who're still free. A gun is all the authority they understand."

"You see our situation pretty clearly," Jessie said.

"I think I do," the Little Shadow Catcher replied. "So if you don't object, Miss Starbuck, I'll just strap on my revolver when we go out to your mine tonight. There are some pretty rough characters among the men who work there."

"If trouble should develop, we'd welcome your help," Jessie said. "Ki has his own weapons, and I intend to put my Colt on before we go to the mine."

"If I'm to go with you, I'd better load my plateholders and put my cameras and the other things I'll need in my wagon," Barry went on. "How soon do you plan to leave?"

Jessie frowned thoughtfully as she said, "Ki and I must go back to the hotel to get ready. A half-hour should be enough for us to do that. Can you be ready to leave that soon?"

"I'm sure I can," he replied. "And I'm used to loading my wagon quickly. I'll try to have all my equipment in it by the time you come back here. I'll want to follow you to the mine, of course."

"Ki and I will be here in a half-hour, then," Jessie said. "Another half-hour or perhaps a bit more should see us at the mine. That should give us all the time we need to get ready before those men start coming in for their midnight meeting."

Chapter 12

As Jessie and Ki left the Dakota Block and turned down Main Street to the hotel, she remarked thoughtfully, "I think Mr. Barry's going to be a good man to have on our side, Ki. I'm sure you noticed how quickly he responds to a new situation."

"There's no doubt about that," Ki agreed. "And if he can help us get the evidence we need tonight, that should end our trouble with Pendergast and Stevens."

They walked on in silence for a few moments, then Jessie said thoughtfully, "You know, Ki, this outfit Elzey Pendergast and Bob Stevens are trying to put together reminds me of the years when we fought the cartel to keep America free. The men who join Pendergast's Friends of the Working Man outfit are letting him make them his slaves."

"You're talking about the agreement they sign when they join?"

Jessie nodded, then went on: "I'm not a lawyer, but that agreement really does make virtual slaves out of the miners! It certainly violates the Constitutional amendment freeing the slaves that President Lincoln got Congress to pass just a little while before he was murdered."

"Well, you and President Hayes got on very friendly terms when you and I were in Washington," Ki said with a smile. "Maybe we ought to send him a telegram and ask him to lend us a few squads of soldiers to break up Pendergast's bunch."

Jessie's smile matched Ki's as she said, "I think we can do the job ourselves. In fact, it looks like we're well on the way, if nothing goes wrong with the plans we have for tonight."

Jessie pulled up her livery horse as they reached the fork of the rutted riverbank road they'd been following since they left Bismarck. Ki and Barry were in Barry's wagon, behind her. Barry also reined in.

She glanced at the sun. Only a narrow strip of blue sky showed now between the riverbank and its bottom rim. Its brightness was dimming perceptibly, and the long strip of gold that its rays cast on the river was beginning to take on the mellow copper tone that came just before sunset.

Turning in her saddle, Jessie called to Barry, "We'll have to stop a little distance from the mine, but by the time we get there it'll be almost fully dark. I'm wondering how much photographic equipment you've brought and how long it's going to take us to move all of it into that old tunnel at the mine and get everything ready."

"How far will we have to carry it?" Barry asked.

"As I remember the lay of the land there, we can angle our horses away from the mine shaft and get behind the big heaps of coal that're piled close to the riverbank for loading," she replied. "It's just a few steps from those piles of coal to the mine shaft. But we're still going to have to carry everything for about a quarter of a mile."

"Then I'm afraid we'll have to make two, maybe three trips to get all my equipment into the mine," Barry said thoughtfully. "But I'm used to carrying my cameras, Miss Starbuck. If you and Ki can carry the film holders and a few boxes of solutions I'll need, I can take care of the cameras."

"How many cameras did you bring?" Ki asked.

"Two, both of them small," Barry told him. "I really didn't know just what to prepare for, so I thought it'd be better to bring too much equipment than too little."

"If each of us makes two trips carrying your gear into the mine, that ought to do the job," Jessie said. "By the time we get there and are ready to move your equipment into it, the office will be closed, the miners on the day shift will be gone and the men who're on the night shift will be down in the mine. I don't think we'll run into any problems."

Barry nodded and Jessie reined ahead, turning her horse to the narrow strip of clear ground between the water's edge and the big stacks of coal that towered above the riverbank in front of them. When they could see the high peaked roof of the mine office towering above the piles of coal, Ki called to Jessie from the wagon seat.

"Suppose you and Mr. Barry go the rest of the way very slowly," he suggested. "I'll go ahead of you and make sure that everything's clear for us to carry Barry's equipment from the wagon to the mine shaft."

Jessie nodded and reined her mount to a slower pace. Ki dropped from the wagon seat to the ground and disappeared between two of the huge heaps of coal. Jessie glanced at the sky. Its blue was deeper now, and the sun's rays showed as only a thin bright line above the horizon across the river. She let her horse move ahead past two more immense heaps of the coal waiting to be shipped, then reined it into the clear space between the next two.

Turning in her saddle, Jessie saw that Barry was following closely behind her. She dismounted, and when the Little Shadow Catcher reined in, she led her horse to the wagon and tethered it to the big rear wheel. Barry came to join her. Jessie had been looking at the photographic equipment in the wagon bed.

"I'm sure it looks like I've emptied my studio, there's so much equipment in there," Barry said. "But I didn't bring a thing that I didn't consider necessary."

"It does look formidable," Jessie agreed. "But we have all the time we need to carry it into the mine."

She broke off as she heard Ki's footsteps crunching lightly on the scattering of coal chips that were strewn on the ground between the big midnight-black piles. Turning to him, she asked, "What did you find?"

"As far as I can tell, there's no one around here," Ki replied. "So we're free to move around pretty much as we please until Pendergast and Stevens and their bunch get here."

Barry was already at the back of the wagon, pulling a tripod out of the wagon bed. He asked, "It's safe to unload, then?"

"I'm sure it is," Ki said. "The office is dark, and the corral's about half-empty. That means the miners on the day shift have gone home and those few horses in the corral belong to the men on the night shift who're down in the mine."

"Good. Then we can start carrying Mr. Barry's equipment down right away," Jessie said. "It shouldn't be too hard to handle, since we're only going down to the first tunnel."

"It won't be," Barry assured her. "A lot of my gear's bulky, but none of it's very heavy except the cameras, and I'd like to take them into the mine myself."

"That's fine," Jessie agreed. "Is there any special order that we need to follow when we bring the things that are still in your wagon?"

Barry shook his head. "The plates are in boxes and the developing trays are all stacked up. So are the film frames, and they'll need to be put on the ground gently. Aside from the plates, the only thing that's heavy are the covered pails that have my solutions in them."

"Ki and I are both used to doing some hard work now and then," Jessie put in. "On my ranch down in Texas everybody works, including me."

"Suppose you take the lantern and one pail, Jessie," Ki suggested. "Mr. Barry is going to be busy setting up his cameras when we get down below, but since there's not any need to hurry, we can take our time carrying in the rest of his equipment."

"As soon as I get to where I'll be working, I'll light one of my safelights and take the red glass frame off of it," Barry volunteered. "Then I won't need the lantern to give me light."

Piece by piece, working silently and steadily, the wagon was emptied of its load. At the dead end of the worked-out first stope, the stack of photographic equipment grew steadily larger until the wagon bed was emptied.

"Why don't you drive the wagon back a little way, Jessie," Ki suggested as they pulled the last boxes of photographic gear out of its bed. "Between these big coal stacks a little way back should be far enough to keep it from being seen by anybody coming here in the dark. I can carry these two boxes by myself."

"You'll need the lantern," Jessie reminded him. "But if you'll stop just inside the stope, I can catch up with you."

"I'll wait," Ki agreed. "It won't take long for us to get everything to the end of the tunnel. Then, while Barry finishes getting ready, you and I can be looking at those papers and the other boxes that I found there. We'll have plenty of time before the miners or Pendergast or Bob Stevens are due to get here."

Ki found that by balancing the last two boxes carefully, he could squat low enough to slip the fingers of one hand into the lantern bail. He did not wait for Jessie, but carried his load to the yawning adit where Barry was standing, waiting. At night the opening seemed less black and dismal; it was only a darker blob than the gloom around it. Stooping until he could no longer feel the pressure of the lantern bail on his fingers, Ki opened his hand to release the light.

"We'll wait for Jessie," he told Barry as he stretched his arms to bring slack to his muscles. "After we've carried this first load to the end of the tunnel, she and I will bring the rest of our gear in while you begin setting up your cameras."

"That won't be a very big job," the little photographer nodded. "And you've said we have enough time to put everything in order before the men I'm to photograph get here."

"Their meeting won't begin until midnight. But

149

there are some things down there that I'm sure Jessie will want you to make images of. Guns and some papers."

"Good. That'll give me a chance to adjust my exposure if I miss it on the first try." At Ki's questioning look, Barry went on to explain: "I'm not quite at home yet with magnesium powder. It's new to the photographic art. I can judge sunlight quite precisely when I'm making an exposure in the daylight, but the magnesium powder's flash is even brighter than the sun."

Before Ki could ask any further questions, Jessie came up to join them. She glanced at the photographic gear that lay around the entrance to the tunnel and said, "That's quite a bit of equipment you've brought, Mr. Barry. We'd better turn to and get it moved so you can be ready before the men we're waiting for start getting here."

Stacked on the floor of the abandoned mine tunnel, Barry's array of photographic gear looked even more imposing than it had when it was being unloaded from the wagon. The little photographer was already working busily at separating the various pieces of equipment into loads one person could carry easily.

"It's going to take a few minutes to get everything sorted out," Barry told Jessie and Ki. "And since we've only got one light, we'll have to stay together until I can get one of my safelights ready."

"Tell us what you intend to carry yourself," Jessie suggested. "Then as soon as you get your own light at the end of the tunnel, Ki and I will bring the rest."

For the next few minutes Barry worked even faster than he had been, until the untidy heap of his gear was separated into three separate groups. Then, with Jessie in the lead carrying a pail of sploshing chemical solution in one hand and the lantern in the other, Ki laden with an unwieldy stack of heavy wooden negative holders topped by one of the safelights, and Barry managing to walk slowly under the load of his two cameras, they moved down the midnight-black tunnel.

Though the distance they had to cover was not great, all three felt that their burdens were growing heavier with each step. They reached a point where the tunnel suddenly began to widen out into a shape like the mouth of a funnel. The tunnel expanded into a large vaultlike chamber. A dozen or so pale patches could now be seen on the floor, and when Jessie reached them with the lantern, they could identify the blobs as big stones. Jessie stopped when she got to them, for ahead in the murky semidarkness she saw that the huge cavernous excavation seemed to end at a black wall.

"Go along either of the sides, Jessie," Ki said. "That's not a wall, even if it does look like one. It's a place where the coal seam spreads wider. The miners left that part of the vein in place there to support the roof."

"Like the places we saw when Bob Stevens was showing us the mine?" Jessie asked.

"Exactly," Ki said. "But this one is just like a wall with a door at each end, and I guess you could call it that. It's really a big oval section of the coal vein that the miners left standing in the center to support the top. They've tunneled on both sides of it to get to the rest of the vein. There's almost as much room behind it as there is where we are now."

"Then that's where you found the guns?"

"Yes. And some boxes of papers as well," Ki replied. "But there's plenty of room on the other side. A

151

lot more space than we'll need to hide in."

While they talked, Jessie had been angling toward one of the tunnel's walls. She saw the opening Ki had told them about and headed for it. Ki and Barry were left for a moment in almost pitch darkness as Jessie walked through the gap carrying the lantern, then they were in the passage and only two or three steps took them through it.

Jessie had stopped just inside the second cavernous excavation. As Ki had remarked, it was nearly as big as the one they'd just left. The light of the lantern was not bright enough to penetrate to its far end. Barry stopped at Ki's side and stood peering toward the end of the second cavern.

"This is the largest darkroom I've ever seen!" he exclaimed as he shook his head in surprise. "But I certainly won't be cramped for space to work in, the way I am in my present one in the Dakota Block!"

"If you'll tell us where you want these pieces of equipment we're carrying," Jessie said. "Ki and I will put them in place and go back for the things we couldn't carry on this trip."

"Give me a moment to set up one of my safelights," he said. "It'll only take a minute to get the cover off, then I'll have light to work by while you're gone."

Barry was true to his time estimate. He took one of the boxy red-paned lights that Ki had been carrying and removed its cover. A small-scaled kerosene lamp had been fixed to the bottom of the square case. He removed the cover, struck a match, and touched it to the wick. The little lamp added its glow to the light of the lantern, and now Jessie could see the boxes of rifles and pistols and other boxes of papers that stood along one side of the cavernous tunnel.

"When you told me you'd found some guns back here, Ki, I didn't realize that you were talking about a whole arsenal!" she exclaimed.

Ki nodded. "I'm surprised myself, but remember that when I came in here yesterday I just got a quick glimpse of this side of the tunnel."

"Why, there are enough guns in those boxes to equip a small army!" Jessie went on.

"That may very well be what Pendergast has in mind," Ki told her. "Enlist a group to take over the mine as a secret headquarters, and then get control of Bismarck."

"Yes," Jessie agreed. "It's a small town, and very isolated. He could enroll and train a bigger force, once he had control of this part of Dakota Territory, and spread out."

"He's putting together a good core of fighting men to work with here," Ki reminded her.

"More than that!" Barry broke in. "The Indians! There are still thousands of their warriors in Canada, you know."

"No, I didn't realize that," Jessie said with a frown. "Texas is a long way off, Mr. Barry. There isn't much talk of Indian fighting there, but here you're still in the middle of the area that Custer and his men were sent to hold when the Indians wiped them out on the Little Bighorn."

"There's still a lot of Indian country left close by, Miss Starbuck," Barry went on. "And I make regular trips into it. I also go to Canada frequently. The Indians don't bother me. They know I'm just 'Icastin-yanka Cikla Hanzi,' the Little Shadow Catcher."

"And I'm sure you've made images of a lot of the chiefs?" Ki asked.

"Yes, indeed. I've made images of Sitting Bull, Gall, Spotted Tail, Rain-in-the-Face, White Eagle, Low Dog and Crow King. They're all still free, up on the British side of the Canadian border. I've asked about their other big chiefs, Four Horns and Red Thunder, but nobody will admit to knowing where they and their fighting men have gone to cover."

"Do the chiefs you've made images of talk with you?" Jessie asked. "Or do they just keep silent?"

"Oh, they talk very freely when I'm around them. And I kept hearing one word so often that I got curious and asked what it was. At first nobody would tell me, but later on I found out it's their common word for war or fighting."

"That would make sense," Ki said. "The Indians were fighting to keep this part of the country for themselves when they defeated Custer."

"And if somebody like Elzey Pendergast was to invite them to join with the bunch he's trying to put together here, I'm sure the Indians would be glad to do exactly that," Jessie said with a frown.

"Oh, the redskins don't make any secret of that," Barry said. "They still consider Dakota Territory to be theirs."

"And from what we've learned about Elzey Pendergast, he's just the kind of man who'd make a deal with them," Jessie said thoughtfully. "Getting control of this mine and the shipyard and the riverboats could be just a part of his plan. I can see now that Elzey Pendergast is a much more dangerous man than we'd taken him to be."

"I think you've gotten down to the core," Ki agreed. "Now we can see that his scheme to organize this Friends of the Working Man could go very far beyond the mine and the other Starbuck properties, Jessie."

"I agree with you, Ki," Jessie said. "He could create a lot of trouble if we've put together a true picture of what he might be planning to do."

"More improbable things have happened," Ki said soberly. "And no matter what our opinion of Pendergast is, he's certainly no fool. A dangerous man, perhaps, but not foolish."

"Can we afford to gamble, Ki?"

"Certainly not," Ki said promptly. "If we don't smash his plans now, the first thing we know he might be planning to get some help from the Indians and trying to capture Bismarck."

"Ki, there are forts close by!" Jessie protested. "One right across the river from Bismarck, one farther upstream, the fort that Joe Foreman was going to, and I don't know how many more."

"He's still recruiting men, Jessie," Ki said. "And I'm sure you're not going to let him get a start at whatever he might be scheming to do. If he succeeds in taking your mine with the help of these Friends of the Working Man he's organizing, who knows how much more he'll try to take?"

"We don't," Jessie said. "Unless there's some kind of evidence in those boxes over there. Ki, let's get busy and bring in the rest of Mr. Barry's equipment. As soon as we do that, we'll just have a look at those boxes while he's putting all his image-making equipment together."

★

Chapter 13

Jessie and Ki made short work of bringing the remainder of David Barry's gear into the old mine tunnel. When they returned, light was outlining the passages at each end of the massive coal pillar that divided the wide chamber. They went through the narrow slit that led into the rear chamber and saw Barry busy at work placing large bottles of his chemical solutions beside the trays that formed a neat line at the base of the pillar.

He did not speak, but looked up and nodded before turning back to the pillar and adjusting the position of one of his boxy safelights that was already propped against the base of the broad pillar. Its red glass cover had been removed and the small lamp inside cast its light across the chamber, creating exaggerated shadows on its walls before its feeble rays were swallowed by the dark tunnel that extended beyond the broad opening.

Two cameras had already been mounted on tripods. They stood near the center of the chamber, ready to be moved into position. Barry finally got the light placed to his satisfaction and stood up.

"I'll want half of those negative carriers you've got there near each side entrance, close to the base of the pillar," he said. "And that box of film goes beside the trays where I can reach it quickly. I'll put the second safelight in place, and the setup job will be finished."

Propped against the wall of coal behind them, a red safelight glowed dimly. The second safelight, still without its red glass cover, shed a brighter light over the spot where the Little Shadow Catcher had stacked the carriers that contained his as yet unexposed negatives.

While Jessie and Ki deposited their loads, Barry moved the second safelight to the point where the chamber narrowed to a tunnel at the back. Then he came up to stand beside Jessie and Ki. His voice showed a bit of anxiety when he spoke.

"I hope there's still enough time left for me to do at least one experimental shot before those men can be expected to start gathering."

Jessie glanced at her little Tiffany watch before replying, "Don't worry, Mr. Barry. It'll be a full hour and a bit more before Pendergast's men are likely to show up. Of course, we'll want to be ready well before then, because some of them are likely to get here early."

"It'll only take me a few minutes to do my experimenting," the photographer went on. "Perhaps you and Ki would be kind enough to stand as models for me?"

"Whatever we can do to help, of course," Jessie assured him. "But if a picture of those boxes of weapons along the wall of the tunnel over there will serve your purpose, I'd rather you used them as your subject."

"Then suppose I include you and Ki in the image, Miss Starbuck," Barry suggested.

"If that's what you'd like to do," Jessie agreed.

"It'll help me judge the exposure if I have you two in the image, even with the tones reversed," Barry said. "Just stand in front of the boxes for a moment while I adjust the focus."

"Will it bother you if we move a bit?" Jessie asked.

"Not at all. Until I get through setting up," Barry assured her.

"Good," Jessie said. "While you're setting up your camera, Ki and I will take two or three of those rifles out of one of the boxes and lean them on either side of wherever you want us to be standing. Your images will be useful evidence if we get these Friends of the Working Man into a court of law."

While Jessie and Ki were arranging the rifles and taking the positions Barry had indicated, the photographer peered at the ground-glass plate at the back of the camera and made a few minor adjustments of the lens before slipping the film-holder into its groove in front of the ground glass.

"Now just move close to the boxes and face the camera," he instructed them. He was walking toward the line of trays as he spoke. He replaced the red cover on the safelight, and the big chamber plunged into a deeper gloom with only the light of the lantern to dispel its almost complete darkness.

Jessie and Ki took the positions he'd indicated while Barry was sprinkling a quantity of magnesium powder into the shallow trough of one of the spark-guns in which it would be ignited. He raised the spark-gun high with one hand and grasped the shutter bulb with the other.

"Now look at me!" Barry called.

A moment after Jessie and Ki froze and were staring at him, Barry triggered a lever which pulled a small flint across a patch of corrugated steel in the spark-gun's magnesium-filled trough. At the same time he squeezed the bulb to trigger the camera's shutter. The click of the shutter release sounded at almost the exact moment when the flint's spark ignited the magnesium powder.

For a fraction of a second a brilliant flash, blinding in its lightning-like intensity, illuminated the semi-obscurity of the underground chamber. Jessie and Ki had blinked instinctively at the flash, but before their eyelids dropped, their images had been caught on the film.

"Very good!" Barry called to them. "Miss Starbuck, if you or Ki will extinguish the lantern, I'll develop the plate at once."

"Will that show you whether or not your exposure was right?" Jessie asked as Ki moved to douse the lantern.

"Oh, yes, indeed," Barry answered. "This magnesium powder is so new to the trade that the only way to learn about it is to expose a few images and study them. When this plate is developed, it will be a guide to me for other exposures."

During the few moments of his conversation with Jessie, Barry had kept busy. Working in the faint reddish glow of the safelights, he'd removed the exposed sheet of film and replaced it with an unexposed sheet. While Barry was doing this, Jessie and Ki had been blinking as their eyes became adjusted to the dim red glow of the safelights.

While they moved closer to get a better look, Barry was inserting the exposed negative into the first tray. Bending forward, Jessie and Ki watched as the developer solution brought a few dark smudges and lines

159

into sight on the film. Slowly the images took on form and even depth.

Although the trays were far too distant from Jessie and Ki to enable them to make out fine details, as the lines and dark blotches darkened they could distinguish their reversed images, the rifles leaning against the boxes of weapons, and even the jagged line made by the muzzles of the guns that were still in the crate.

Their span of observation was brief, for Barry soon gave a small exclamation of satisfaction and lifted the plate from the tray holding the developing solution. He doused it in the second tray for a moment or two, holding it delicately by one corner, then slipped it into the third tray. He covered the tray with the dark slide from the negative holder and stood up.

"Just as soon as I put an unexposed plate in the carrier, we can light the lantern again," Barry said. "The negative image will be fixed by then. I'm very well satisfied with the way it looks, Miss Starbuck, but you won't be able to see it at its best until I make a positive image of it on paper."

"I suppose that will be when we get back to your studio?" Jessie asked.

"Yes, a coated plate must be put in the developer just as soon as possible," Barry replied. "Then it's rinsed and goes into the acid solution that hardens the image and fixes it permanently. Just a quick dip in water will rinse off most of the acid, and the plate can be given a more thorough washing later."

"Watching you at work is very interesting," Jessie told Barry. "And I can see now why the Indians call you the Shadow Catcher. But Ki and I have our own work to do. While we're putting this room back in order, will you make images of those guns in their boxes? If it's possible, I'd also like for you to make images of some of the papers that are in one of the boxes. Can you do that, Mr. Barry?"

"Oh, quite easily. It'll take only a few minutes. And I won't develop any more plates until we have the remaining images you've said you want, of the men who'll be in the other big chamber."

"And that might be easier to talk about than to do," Ki put in. "How can you operate two cameras, Mr. Barry?"

"I can't be in two places at once, though I often wish I could," Barry said with a smile. "But after giving it some thought, I've worked out a plan."

"One to solve the problem?" Jessie asked.

Barry nodded. "Yes. When I've fired a charge of magnesium powder, the men in that other chamber will be looking toward my camera. I'll have the second camera ready, and I'll ask you to stand beside it and a half-step in back of it. Lift the powder tray as high as possible and press the plunger of the cable. Ki, if you'll do the same thing at the other camera, that's all you need to do."

"I'm sure I can handle that much of a photographer's job," Ki agreed.

Barry went on: "Now, Miss Starbuck, while Ki's taking the second image, I'd like for you to be standing beside me with a fresh plate holder and the jar of magnesium powder."

"That sounds simple enough," Jessie said. "But I suppose there's more to come."

"There is," Barry told her. "As soon as I've made the first image, I'll hand you the magnesium trough. I'll take out the exposed plate and we'll exchange plate holders. I'll slide the plate holder you've been holding into the camera, and while I'm doing that I'll ask you to pour some magnesium powder into its trough and hand it back to me quickly. If everything goes as I hope it will, I'll get still another image."

"Which will give us three images, and in two of them the faces of the men will be showing clearly," Jessie said.

"Exactly," Barry agreed. "Any faces that might be obscured in one of them should be clear in another."

"Now that you've explained your plan, it doesn't sound quite as simple as I'd imagined," Jessie said with a smile. "But it really shouldn't be too hard to do."

"Good!" Barry exclaimed. "Now that we know what each of us is to take care of, we can go ahead and finish any other details that need our attention."

"Yes," Jessie agreed. "And by the time you've made a few images of those papers, I have a hunch that some of the men who're going to attend the meeting will be showing up."

For the next few minutes Barry moved like a whirling dervish as he made exposures of the documents which Jessie and Ki took from the box. Then he devoted himself to readying his cameras and going over his earlier instructions to make sure that both Jessie and Ki understood the routines they must follow for their scheme to be successful. He was in the midst of one of his repetitions when the murmur of voices trickled in from the chamber beyond the broad coal-post barrier. As the voices grew louder the blackness at each end of the dividing pillar began shading to a yellowish luminosity, indicating that the new arrivals were carrying a lantern.

"Hush!" Jessie whispered. "And please douse your red lights quickly, Mr. Barry! Someone's coming into the tunnel on the other side of the pillar, and they may decide to come back here!"

Ki blew out the lantern's wick while Jessie was warning Barry. Instead of blowing out the wicks that still burned in his red-glassed safelights, Barry turned them and pressed their glass fronts to the pillar's wall. Only a few toothpick-thin pinpoints of barely-visible red gleams showed where they stood.

Jessie's eyes and Ki's were already accustomed to dimness, and they picked their way with silent care to the edges of the broad dividing pillar. The yellowish glow of lantern light was now outlining the tunnel beyond their safety barrier. The voices grew steadily louder as the light in the tunnel became brighter. Only a few moments passed before the listeners in the shielding darkness could make out a scattered word or two of the invisible conversationalists. None of the few wisps of sound they heard had any meaning.

After they'd listened for a few more ticks of time, Jessie nudged Ki and pressed her mouth close to his ear to whisper, "There's no mistaking that pompous voice, Ki. It's Pendergast."

"Yes," Ki breathed. "And I'm sure now it's Bob Stevens who's with him."

"If they decide to come back into this part of the tunnel, we won't have much chance of keeping them from seeing us."

"No. All we can do is hope that luck will be on our side, Jessie."

Before she could reply, Pendergast's deep booming tones suddenly became intelligible and the dancing shadows from the light he or Stevens was carrying grew still. Pendergast was saying, "... enough men to get rid of both the Starbuck woman and the chink

163

that's with her, if we have to. But if they just dropped out of sight without any reason, it'd raise a whopping big fuss all over the country very soon after they were missed. Jessie Starbuck's name's too damn well known in too many places to risk any sort of hullabaloo and have God knows who or how many people coming here to look for her."

"At least she hasn't stumbled onto what our plans are yet," Stevens said. "And I'll work as fast as I can to convince Jessie that everything's all right here."

"I still think you made your first mistake when you told her about the Friends," Pendergast said. "You ought to have let her find out about them herself."

"And I still say you're wrong!" Stevens retorted. "Sure, she'd have found out for herself if I hadn't told her, and the next thing you know she'd have begun to suspect that I might be mixed up in whatever's going on. She'd be sure to think there was something wrong with me because I hadn't mentioned them right off! Then she'd've begun wondering why and started digging around. We—"

"That's enough, damn it!" Pendergast snapped. "I'll admit you might be right. She's a snoopy damned bitch, pokes into everything. What'd she say when you talked to her today?"

"I didn't see her today. She and the chink was supposed to come out here to the mine, but they never did show up. My guess is that she was nosying around the shipyard, asking questions about it and the river-boats."

Pendergast's voice showed his anger as he asked, "You mean you haven't put our men to keeping tabs on her? I want to know what she's doing every minute! Her and the chink both!"

"I tried to get hold of Lefty Blake, but he wasn't anyplace to be found," Stevens answered. "Neither was Jeff Carson. And I sure wasn't going to put one of the new recruits on a job like that. I wanted somebody I was sure we could trust."

"Well, you showed good sense in that," Pendergast grunted. "Now, let's go over what we want to tell these fellows who're supposed to meet us here."

"They're all new recruits," Stevens said. "And all of 'em have signed the roster and taken the oath, but they still don't know how to pull more of their kind into the Friends."

"How many are there?"

"Maybe a dozen, give or take one or two. I thought about bringing some of the other men in, a few that've been with us from the start. Then I remembered that the last time we did that the ones that've been with us a long time kept butting in when you or me was trying to talk. I figured it'd be better if we just let the new ones get acquainted with each other first."

"That's not too bad an idea," Pendergast agreed. "Now what do we need to take care of before those new men start getting here?"

"Nothing I can think of," Stevens answered. "The stuff on the other side of that support pillar's all right, I looked at it yesterday just to be sure. When the time's right tonight, I'll go back and get the books and the forms and give the new men their guns."

"We've got damn near enough recruits to start moving," Pendergast went on. "The word ought to get back from the reservations up north and in Canada about the redskins joining up with us. Old Bent Nose has been working hard, trying to get them to have a shot at getting back what used to be theirs."

"You really think the Indians will fight again?" Stevens asked. "There's a lot more soldiers in Dakota Territory now than there were when they whipped Custer."

"They'll fight," Pendergast assured him. "With the guns I'm buying for them, they can take on a lot bigger bunch than Custer's troop was and still come out on top."

"Then you—" Stevens stopped short as the sound of other voices could be heard from the tunnel that led to the big underground chamber. He and Pendergast said nothing for a moment, then Stevens went on: "That'll be our new recruits."

"Put the lantern up on that little shelf behind where we'll be standing, then," Pendergast said. "When I'm talking to a bunch of green ones like these fellows are, it helps if I can watch their faces."

For a moment the light trickling into the cavern from the other side of the coal pillar grew brighter, then it faded as Stevens placed it where Pendergast mentioned. In its new position high on the pillar the lantern created a triangle of deep obscurity at the ends of the passageways along the side walls.

"They couldn't've picked a place for that lantern that would help us more," Jessie whispered to Ki and Barry. "It's dark enough at each side now for us to move your cameras and put them where you'll be sure of getting images that will take in most of the other half of the tunnel."

"You've learned a great deal about image-making in a very short time, Miss Starbuck," Barry whispered in reply. "I was just about to say that myself."

Moving slowly and silently, the small noises they made going unnoticed on the other side of the pillar, they shifted the cameras into the shadows. Barry, standing on tiptoe with the ease which short-statured persons acquire, inspected the ground-glass backs of each camera after it had been set in place and made a few quick adjustments of their lenses.

"We can put the film in place, now," he whispered as he rejoined Jessie and Ki. "When do you want me to make my exposures, Miss Starbuck?"

"Wait until the men are all in place and interested in whatever it is that Pendergast will be telling them," she said. Her voice was pitched to the same almost-inaudible key as Barry's. "I don't want to disturb the men on the other side of that pillar until I've heard what Pendergast has to tell them. And I hope we can get a good clear image of Pendergast's face. I want to find out more about him."

"I'll do my best to get a good image of him, then," Barry promised. "But you must remember that once the first magnesium powder's gone off, those men on the other side will be milling around, and when they move the images will be blurred. Our exposures must be made very quickly, one after the other."

"I'll remember," Jessie promised. "Now all we have to do is wait."

★

Chapter 14

Standing beside the camera tripod, with Ki close at hand holding the tray of magnesium powder, Jessie concentrated her attention on the jumble of voices that filled the tunnel on the opposite side of the pillar. From the occasional snatches of conversation that reached her ears clearly, she could judge what was going on: Pendergast and Stevens were mixing with the new arrivals, getting acquainted. At last Pendergast's voice rose above the babble.

"All right, you men!" he called. "It's time to get down to the business that's brought us here! All of you find a place to sit, and we'll get started!"

Gradually the jumble of sounds died away. Then Stevens's voice, higher-pitched then Pendergast's, broke the silence.

"I guess all of you know that we're here to tell you more about the Friends of the Working Man," he began. "Now, all of you are working men. I guess you know how badly we need a few friends to help us get what's due us from the bosses that give us a few dollars every month for a lot of hard work. Well, Mr. Pendergast thinks the same thing. I don't suppose there's more than two of three of you who's met him before. So I'm going to step aside while he tells you what it's all about."

A stir of voices broke the silence that had settled over the men on the opposite side of the pillar while Stevens was talking. Then the darkness in which Jessie and Ki were standing was banished by a burst of brilliant light.

"Make your image, Jessie!" Ki said in the darkness that had settled down as quickly as it had been broken. "Hurry!"

Jessie pressed the plunger of the shutter release. At the same time Ki's fingers closed on the trigger that set off the magnesium powder.

Again the tunnel was flooded with light for a fraction of a second while the brilliant burst of magnesium powder burned away. The voices of the men beyond the pillar added to the confusion of sounds that now filled the tunnel. Though she was still half-blinded by the overpowering burst of light, Jessie dropped the shutter-release cable and drew her Colt. The revolver's muzzle had barely cleared its holster when Jessie was blinded by the new glare that marked Barry's second exposure.

After the three brilliant flashes of magnesium powder, the lantern's yellow glow in the section of tunnel where the Friends of the Working Man had been meeting seemed feeble and dim. The men who'd been sitting on the stones were on their feet now, milling around, most of them still as powerless as Jessie was to see anything in the glowing yellow lantern light.

As they milled around, one of them kicked the lantern over in his flounderings. Its chimney shattered with a tinkle of breaking glass as the wick glared for a second or so before it faltered and faded out. Voices rang through the midnight blackness.

Pendergast's booming shout broke through the chatter. "Hold your places, you men! Whoever flashed those lights can't get away from us!"

"We'll catch 'em and they'll pay!" Stevens seconded.

None of the new recruits gave any indication that they heard the commands.

"Let's get the hell outa here!" one of them yelled.

"This damn tunnel's caving in!" another called. "All of us better get out while we still got a chance to!"

"Every man for himself!" a third shouted.

Boots were already thunking on the packed dirt floor as the panicked men Stevens had been addressing began running toward the tunnel's exit.

Pendergast's loud voice rose above the din. "Wait, damn it!" he commanded. "Nobody's been hurt! You men come on back here! We've got to find out who it is trying to break up our meeting!"

Stevens's lighter voice followed almost before Pendergast's command had died away. "Those fellows won't stop!" he snapped. "I'll go after them and try to get them to come back!"

"Damn it, I'm not staying here in the dark by myself to go up face who knows what!" Pendergast's voice was almost a shout. "We'll both go after them!"

Almost before the flash of Barry's second magnesium charge died away, Jessie had realized that her original plan was now completely useless. A half-dozen fragments of alternative moves flashed through her mind, instant memories of past encounters with her old antagonists who'd tried to wrest away segments of her inheritance. She realized at once that her most important objective must be to get out of the mine with the evidence of Pendergast's scheme preserved on Barry's photographic negatives.

Turning to Ki, she said quickly, "Go help Barry, Ki. I'm going to drive these men out. It's got to be done if we're going to get out ourselves."

"What do you want us to do?" Ki asked.

"Hide his photographic gear, especially his cameras and the holders with the images in them."

"Where, Jessie? There isn't —"

"Carry as much as you can back toward the end of the tunnel. But first bring me a—no, bring two rifles, Ki. One for me and one for yourself. I left my Winchester at the hotel. We'll need a box of shells, too. Your *shuriken* won't carry far enough to be effective if we're chasing men on horseback."

Ki nodded. "I know their limits, Jessie. And even though I'd use them because they're silent and mysterious to those men, a rifle's the weapon I'll need now."

"Pendergast's carrying a lantern," Jessie went on. "But if my guess is right, he'll leave it here. But we'd better move fast now, Ki. Just be sure that Barry knows what to do and find out whether he's going to need any help."

"I'll tell him we'll be back in a few minutes."

In the dimness behind the massive pillar, Ki found Barry hunkered down behind the pillar, bending over the developing trays in the faint reddish gleam cast by the safelight.

"I heard all the ruckus you and Miss Starbuck stirred up," the Little Shadow Catcher said. "I'd've joined in with you, but it was more important for me

171

to get this film developed right away. I've got to do it at once, before the images on it fade."

"Pendergast and his recruits are on the run," Ki told him. "Jessie and I want to go after them while they're still in a panic. Do you mind working alone down here?"

"Of course not!" Barry replied without taking his eyes off the trays. "I'd join you in a minute if I didn't have to get my images developed."

"I'm going to put a loaded rifle by you," Ki said. "If you get through before Jessie and I are back, you might go along the tunnel to the shaft mouth and keep anybody from coming in here."

"I've got my pistol, Ki," Barry replied. "And I know how to use it. But put the rifle here anyhow."

Ki nodded and went on: "We'll need the lantern to light our way along the tunnel. And we'll have to borrow your wagon horse, if you don't object."

"Take it, of course. When I finish developing the negatives, I'll just take the red covers off the safelights."

Ki nodded. His eyes had adjusted to the obscurity by now, and he found the lantern quickly. Realizing that lighting it would ruin Barry's work, Ki looped the lantern's bail over his arm and went to the boxes of rifles. He pulled out two of them and scrabbled through the ammunition box until he found shells that matched the caliber of the rifles. Then he hurried through the passageway and started back to join Jessie.

A few steps along the black gloom of the tunnel after it narrowed convinced Ki that the advantage of being able to see instead of having to move slowly outweighed the risk of carrying a light. He stopped long enough to strike one of his Beecher matches and light the lantern.

Picking up the rifles and ammunition, he moved along the tunnel, but had taken only a few steps into the blackness when Jessie's voice sounded ahead.

"Here I am, Ki! Those men aren't out of the tunnel yet. I can still hear one of them yelling now and then."

"They've got a little edge on us, though."

"We're used to catching up, Ki! Let's go!"

A few more quick steps brought Ki to Jessie's side. He asked, "Have Pendergast and Stevens and the men gotten out of the mine by now?"

"Not all of them. But I've been going very slowly, feeling my way. They've moved faster; either Pendergast or Stevens has a lantern."

"So have we, now. If we move fast, maybe we can catch up with them."

They were moving ahead along the tunnel as they spoke, Ki holding the lantern high. They'd covered only a few yards when a shot barked from the darkness beyond the small patch of light cast by the lantern. It's chimney shattered with a tinkling of broken glass and the wick guttered and went out. Jessie and Ki were left standing in total blackness.

Another blast of gunfire echoed through the tunnel and this time the slug screeched along the stone formation that roofed the tunnel at that point. The rasping sound ended abruptly as the bullet reached the end of the stone arch and plowed into one of the crusted areas of time-hardened earth that stretched between the expanses of rock.

A thud sounded at Jessie's feet. She slid one foot along the floor until it was stopped by something heavy and bulky. Bending down, her hand encountered cold earth and colder stones in a heap piled on the tunnel's floor.

"That shot missed us, but it might have been intentional," she told Ki as she felt the tunnel floor with her boot tip to guide herself around the heap of rock-studded soil that was piled on it. "That shot brought down a chunk of the ceiling. They may be planning to keep pouring bullets into it until it collapses!"

"We'll have to move faster, then!" Ki said. "Or give up the idea of chasing Pendergast and Bob Stevens until we can help Barry get out of here."

"No!" Jessie said. "Even if the tunnel should cave in, we can hire help in Bismarck to come dig him out before he suffocates. Right now it's more important to catch up with Pendergast and Stevens!"

"Yes, you're right," Ki agreed. "Let's push on!"

They forged ahead, Jessie on one side of the tunnel, Ki on the other, both of them feeling their way along its sides. The distance they covered in the pitch darkness seemed to stretch to eternity, for a few scattered shots from the fleeing men whistled past them or plowed into the sides or top of the old tunnel.

Several times they stumbled over heaps of loose dirt and stone that the gunfire had jarred loose from the roof or sides of the cavernous aging excavation. Actually, only a few minutes had passed following the first shots before the faint sounds of shouting voices reached their ears from the blackness ahead.

"We're closing the gap!" Jessie exclaimed. "If our luck holds out, we might make it to the end of this tunnel before all of them get away!"

"If we can hear them, it won't be long before we can see them, too," Ki agreed.

A dozen paces farther they saw a vague blob of

lesser darkness, and as they hurried along it grew a bit brighter. Soon the sound of men's shouting voices began to trickle along the tunnel, though the distance was still too great for them to make out any words. The voices were only faint sounds that trickled down the shaft that was now becoming more visible with each step they made, but as they forged steadily ahead, they heard a fleeting word or two, usually a choice bit of profanity.

They reached a point where the blob of light took shape and form. Ahead they could make out the shadows of the steps cut into the walls of the mine's vertical shaft, steps that gave access to the lower tunnels as well as to the surface. Soon they were within a half-dozen paces of the shaft. Now they could see the steps clearly as well as being able to see each other once again.

Ki closed his free hand over Jessie's wrist. "Wait here, Jessie," he said. "Let me go ahead. My dark clothes will keep me from being seen easily."

"No!" she replied. "I intend to go with you, Ki!"

"But I can make sure it's safe for us to go up the shaft!"

"Safe or not, we're going up to the surface together!"

Ki heard the firmness in Jessie's voice and recognized that any further discussion would be useless.

"All right," he nodded. "But just let me lead the way. My *ninjutsu* will give us a little edge."

"Go first, then," Jessie nodded. "But hurry, before they can reach the hitch rail and get to their horses!"

Chapter 15

Laying the rifle on the step he was standing on, Ki
brought up one foot and planted it on the next step.
Bending forward until his shoulders were no higher
than his hips, Ki levered himself up to the last step.
Then he brought up his head and shoulders inch by
inch until he was sure that he'd have a clear view
across the open area between the adit and the office
building.

Cautiously, Ki raised his head. One thin pointed tip
of the waning moon was visible above the building's
roof. The big structure cast its shadow almost to the
hitch rail. Shouts and the occasional thud of bootsoles
on the hard-beaten earth were still sounding from the
cleared area that stretched from the mine's entrance to
the building that housed its office. On that broad
stretch of ground, he saw the dark shapes of the men
fleeing from the shaft. Two or three of the men who'd
left the mine were within a few yards of the tethered
animals, the rest were straggling behind in a spread-
out group.

There was no doubt about their objective; the men
were heading for the hitch rail, which stood at the far

corner of the office building. In the darkness it was impossible for Ki to count them, and between the need for concealment while in the mine tunnel and the dense gloom of its depths neither he nor Jessie had been able to make a tally. Ki did not worry about the possibility that the fleeing runners had left a rear guard, nor did he consider the odds that were so heavily against him. He knew now that his pursuit of the runners would be made over familiar ground.

A rustle just behind him reached Ki's ears and told him that Jessie had stepped behind him. He turned to speak to her.

"They're getting away, but they aren't worth chasing. I can't tell one from the other of them, Jessie, and I'm sure that even in the dark I'd recognize Pendergast and Stevens. But they're not in that bunch, and the two of them are the only ones we're interested in."

"That's right," she agreed. "The rest of them don't matter a bit."

From the impenetrable blackness of the office building's shadow a rifle barked. The slug raised a burst of dust less than a yard from Jessie and Ki. She raised her rifle, but Ki closed his hand around its action and pushed the weapon down, then grasped her arm and pulled her into a crouch.

"Not yet, Jessie," he said.

"But either Pendergast or Bob Stevens must've fired that shot, Ki!" she protested. "That means they must've seen us! And as soon as they see one of us again, they'll be sure to make another try!"

"Of course. But in that shadow where they are now, you'd be lucky to hit either one. Stay here for a minute or so longer. And keep low. *Ninjutsu* will get me to where I can see if they're really in that big shadow around the office building."

"They've got rifles, Ki," Jessie said. "Before you get halfway there—"

"*Ninjutsu*, Jessie," Ki broke in. "And if I see them, I've got my *shuriken*."

Remembering the many other occasions when Ki's martial arts skills had saved them from disaster, Jessie nodded.

"Go ahead," she agreed. "I know you won't make a target of yourself, and I'll cover you as best I can."

Before she'd finished speaking, Ki was levering himself out of the shaft. He was too greatly skilled in the *ninja* arts of self-concealment on open ground to make a mistake at this point. He bent forward slowly as he levered himself out of the mine shaft and began belly-crawling toward the office building. When he reached its shadows, his black-clad form vanished and Jessie strained her eyes in vain trying to follow his movements.

Though Jessie had learned more than a little about *ninjutsu* from Ki, her skill at the ancient Japanese art of moving with virtual invisibility was not as great as his. The longer she watched now, the greater her worry grew. At last she left the protection of the mine shaft and set out to follow him.

Slowly and carefully, stretched flat on his belly, Ki pushed himself forward. He moved only his sandaled toes to propel himself, and advanced so slowly that he might have been a motionless shadow among the many other pools of black that showed on the rock-strewn ground he was crossing.

He covered almost a quarter of the distance that lay

between the mouth of the shaft and the office building when a shot rang out behind him, from the mine shaft. Stopping immediately, Ki twisted to look back, but he'd completed only a small segment of the turn that was needed to see the shaft when two close-spaced rifle shots sounded from the gloom of the building's base.

Neither of the whistling bullets came close to him. Both landed with angry spats at the edge of the shaft. By the time they'd hit, Ki had completed his turn, and his darkness-dilated eyes caught no sign of Jessie. Stretching straight again, he resumed his steady progress, but had advanced only a few feet when the sharp crack of a rifle shot broke the stillness. With the rifle's bark a red flash of muzzle-blast cut through the darkness on the side of the office building farthest away from Ki's position.

Puzzled, Ki stopped and lay motionless. Most of the men who'd been in the tunnel had reached the hitch rail by now. The area around it was a jumble of confused motion, and Ki seized the opportunity he now saw. Rising to his feet, he began running toward the fleeing men. He'd covered only a few yards when a rifle shot sounded behind him. Turning, Ki peered through the increasingly bright moonglow and saw Jessie running toward him.

Another rifle barked and its muzzle-flash cut a red streak in the black shadow that concealed the near end of the building. Its slug kicked up dust only a yard from Jessie's running feet.

She was moving in a zigzag now, veering from side to side to make herself a more elusive target. Once again the rifleman concealed by the blackness tried to cut Jessie down, but this time the slug sailed past Ki's head. He dropped flat and waited until Jessie reached him, then leaped to his feet, caught her by the arm, and stopped her.

"Lay flat!" he told her, pulling Jessie with him as he dropped to the ground again. "I'm sure that Pendergast and Bob Stevens are the ones who're sniping at us from behind the office building, but there's somebody at the far end of it who seems to be trying to help us. He can't reach them with his shots, though."

"I know," Jessie replied. "I've been watching as best I could while I was trying to follow you. But I don't understand what's going on. There's nobody in Bismarck who even knows where we are!"

Once again the night was broken by gunfire, another shot from the rifleman hidden in the shadows of the building. Jessie raised her rifle and still lying prone triggered off a shot at their enemies. The dull thud of the slug hitting the wall told them that her bullet had been wasted.

Even before the *thunk* of Jessie's slug had died away, two quick shots sounded from the shadows of the building. The dark bulks of two running men suddenly broke from the gloom and were outlined in the dim moonglow. Their pistols barked, breaking the silence that had settled after the last exchange of gunfire.

Jessie and Ki moved with the fast reactions honed by the many times they'd faced similar dangers. Ki's *shuriken* made a silver streak through the moonlit night just as Jessie's rifle cracked. The black form of one of the men who'd run from the concealing shadows was thrust backward by the impact of Jessie's bullet. The other lurched forward, his hands going to his throat as he toppled to the ground. Then both of the fleeing men lay sprawled and motionless.

No words were needed between Jessie and Ki. They started at a dead run toward the black shapes huddled in the moonlight. They'd taken only a few steps when still a third man emerged from the shadows. He was holding his hands above his head, a revolver was in one hand.

"Hold your fire, Miss Starbuck!" he called. "I'm on your side!"

Ki's arm was already drawn back, a *shuriken* in his hand ready to be sent in its deadly spinning arc. He did not throw it, but held his arm poised in readiness.

"Who are you?" Jessie called to the man who'd appeared so unexpectedly. He was still standing with his hands raised, his revolver pointed to the night sky.

"Allan Pinkerton, Miss Starbuck," the newcomer replied. "You'll recall that we met in Washington some years ago at a reception in the White House."

"Allan Pinkerton, the head of the Secret Service?" Jessie asked.

"Of course. And may I please lower my arms now? I'm not used to holding this position and my pistol's getting heavier every minute."

"Do you recognize his voice?" Ki whispered to Jessie.

"I can't be sure yet," she answered. "But I don't think there'd be anyone in Dakota Territory who'd be trying to pass themselves off as him, or who'd know about the time we got acquainted in Washington." It was Jessie's turn to raise her voice now. She called, "Please give your arms a rest, Mr. Pinkerton. But I'm sure you won't object if we step into the moonlight, and I'd better tell you that I won't lower my rifle until we get close enough for me to see your face."

"No objection at all, Miss Starbuck," he replied as he let his arms fall to his sides and started toward Jessie and Ki. "And I congratulate you on being so cautious."

Jessie and Ki took the two or three steps that brought them into the brightening moonlight. The man in the shadows lowered his arms and started walking slowly toward them. As they moved closer, they could see that he wore the rough clothing of a mine worker and had the full but frazzled and unkempt beard that was favored by most of the miners. Jessie studied his face and movements as he emerged from the gloom.

"Yes, of course," she said when she got her first clear view in the dim moonlight. "I recognize you now, Mr. Pinkerton. That is, except for your beard. It was a bit more closely trimmed when we met in the White House."

"That's part of the disguise I've had to use while I was here in Bismarck," Pinkerton told her. He was holstering his revolver as he spoke. "My face is getting too well known these days. But I've been trying to recapture that man calling himself Pendergast for almost a year now. I was ready to close in on him tonight. I joined his Friends of the Working Man to get evidence that would allow me to arrest him."

"He was a wanted criminal, then?" Ki asked.

"Very badly wanted, for using the United States mail to defraud and for at least two murders that he committed back East," Pinkerton nodded. "One of the men he killed was a Secret Service operative; that's what brought me into the case. And he's swindled honest working men out of thousands of dollars."

"Then his Friends of the Working Man was just a

way to cheat the miners here out of their money?" Jessie asked.

"He's been trying to imitate the Knights of Labor, which is a legitimate union," Pinkerton explained. "But Pendergast—I'll keep calling him that for convenience—just collected thousands of dollars in dues and put the money in his own pocket."

"Now I can understand what happened here," Jessie said slowly. "Pendergast bribed my manager, Bob Stevens. Or perhaps he cajoled Bob to join him by making promises that he had no intention of keeping. I don't suppose we'll ever know what really went on between them."

"Except for one thing," Ki added. "Now we're sure that Pendergast won't cheat anyone else."

A crunch of gravel drew their eyes from the sprawled form of the man who'd called himself Pendergast. They turned to see a square of white light approaching from the direction of the mine shaft.

"Why, it's Mr. Barry!" Jessie exclaimed. "We've forgotten that he was back in the mine!"

"Barry," Pinkerton said thoughtfully. "The photographic artist? The one the Indians call the Little Shadow Catcher? I've been hearing about him ever since I got to Bismarck."

Barry called, "Miss Starbuck? I've been wondering what happened to you. I heard the miner's meeting break up, but I couldn't leave my work to help you. My images are all developed and all of them look very good indeed."

"That's fine," Jessie replied. "And I'll be looking forward to seeing them after you've transferred them to paper."

"Will tomorrow be soon enough?" Barry asked.

"I'm just a bit too tired to do any more work tonight."

"Tomorrow's fine," Jessie replied. "Ki and I will stop by your studio tomorrow morning, and I'll pay your bill and pick up the images. We're a bit tired, too, and I'm sure Mr. Pinkerton is as well."

Standing in the bow of the *Nellie Peck*, Jessie and Ki watched the rippling bow wave curving past as the riverboat began to gain speed, aided by the downriver current.

"I'm glad we finally got everything cleared up," Jessie said with a sigh. "Even if Clarence Moorehead hasn't had any experience managing the mine or the shipyard, he's been in the office long enough to handle his new job. And I think we're doing the right thing by going home. I'm glad we decided not to extend this trip."

"At least you're taking some souvenirs back home this time," Ki told her. "The images Mr. Barry made of you are excellent."

"I'm pleased with them," Jessie agreed. "And whenever I look at one, it will always remind me of the Little Shadow Catcher."

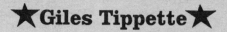